He knew he'd caught her and he wasn't about to let her go.

"On the contrary, I don't think of myself at all." For the first time he was able to think of something other than the accident that ultimately led him to this woman. "What I do find myself thinking of – quite against my will –" he admitted, lowering his voice to almost a whisper, "is you."

"I didn't think that was possible."

"There was a definite connection last Wednesday. When we kissed –"

"When you kissed me," she corrected.

"You're ignoring the important part."

"Which is?" she challenged.

"That you kissed me back. And that there *were* sparks."

"Look, Malone, get this through your head. I am not interested in having an affair."

Ian's mouth curved. She was a challenge. He'd always loved a challenge, even though he knew that this time he should be backing off

Available in April 2008
from Mills & Boon®
Special Edition

Romancing
the Teacher

MARIE
FERRARELLA

MILLS & BOON

Pure reading pleasure

First published in Great Britain 2008
by Harlequin Mills & Boon Limited,
Eton House, 18-24 Paradise Road, Richmond, Surrey TW9 1SR

© Marie Rydzynski Ferrarella 2007

ISBN: 978 0 263 86040 5

23-0408

Harlequin Mills & Boon policy is to use papers that are
natural, renewable and recyclable products and made from
wood grown in sustainable forests. The logging and
manufacturing processes conform to the legal environmental
regulations of the country of origin.

Printed and bound in Spain
by Litografia Rosés S.A., Barcelona

Dear Reader,

The title of this book was originally "And Promises To Keep." It comes from an old Robert Frost poem that I've always loved, especially the line about "And miles to go before I sleep" because it's the story of my life. I always feel as if I have miles to go before I sleep and along those miles, promises to keep. In the case of this book, the hero, Ian, unconsciously has promises to keep. The promises, or actually promise he needs to keep is living up to his full potential. Living up to the promise of four lives instead of just one, the lives of his parents and his sister as well as his own. He needs to prove to himself that there was a reason why he survived that terrible accident, rather than died with the rest of his family on that fateful day. Lisa Kittridge comes into his life by accident and helps him get beyond his feelings of guilt so that he can finally keep his promise: to live life to the fullest.

As always, I wish you someone to love who loves you back. Everything else is a distant second.

Marie Ferrarella

To Rocky,
for twelve years of
love and loyalty and
a bunch of sleepless nights.

MARIE FERRARELLA

This *USA TODAY* bestselling and RITA® Award winning author has written over one hundred and fifty novels for Mills & Boon® books, some under the name Marie Nicole. Her romances are beloved by fans worldwide.

Chapter One

When he realized that the darkness was of his own making because his eyes were shut, Ian Malone struggled to pry them open.

The world was a blur.

Inch by inch, he became aware that the darkness that he now saw was the natural kind. It was the warm, cocooning darkness of night, not the hazy dark world of unconsciousness he had tumbled into what seemed like only a moment ago.

Not the netherworld either.

Damn.

His surroundings came into focus in almost comic slow motion. Snippets gradually telegraphed themselves through his brain. His fingers were no longer wrapped around the steering wheel of his car. In fact, he wasn't in his car at all.

Somewhere in the distance was the ever-annoying sound of crickets looking for one another. Looking to mate. Looking for a family.

Good luck with that, he thought sarcastically.

Ian groaned as he tried to raise his head. He felt as if an anvil weighed it down, like what you saw in Saturday morning cartoons.

Did they still have Saturday morning cartoons? He'd stopped watching when he was ten. When he stopped being a kid.

His head was too heavy. He let it drop back down. It made contact with something damp. He was too out of it to care.

He became aware that someone was standing over him. Someone wide enough to block out what light was coming from the moon, breathing as if the smog was battling for possession of his windpipe—and winning. Whoever it was sounded a little like Darth Vader.

Or was that the grim reaper hovering over him, checking for signs of life? Finally there to collect his debt.

God, he hoped so.

"I'm not dead yet, am I?" Ian's mouth felt like baked cotton as he formed the question. The traces of regret in his voice were punctuated with another groan.

The face glaring down at him was craggy and appeared worn. And annoyed. The man wore a uniform of some sort.

Black.

No, dark blue.

Of course, the police. It was a police uniform. Sooner or later, the police always came to the scene of an accident or a disaster, didn't they? Sometimes they came too late, he thought. Like the other time.

The anvil shifted from his head to his chest, pressing down. But nothing was there.

The policeman leaning over him frowned in disgust as he shook his head. "No, you're not dead yet. Better luck next time, buddy."

"I'll hold you to that," Ian said, biting back another groan. He continued to lay there. His head felt as if it would split in two. For all he knew, his body already had.

The officer straightened up, one hand braced against his spine as he examined the wreckage. His car was a mangled scrap of machinery intimately locked in an eternal waltz with the bark of a coral tree.

The officer took off his hat and scratched his balding head.

"You'd think a man who could afford a fine machine like that would have more sense than to go driving around with Johnnie Walker as a companion."

But bottles of Johnnie Walker were far in Ian's

past. That had been his grandfather's poison of choice, not his.

"It was vodka, not whiskey," Ian corrected hoarsely. "And definitely not enough to get me in this state." That had been the fault of his medication, he thought. Maybe he'd been a little careless, taking too much because of what day it was. These days, they had a medicine for everything. Everything but the guilt that came with each breath he took.

Because he could take a breath. And they couldn't. Not for a very long time.

With effort, Ian pulled his elbows in against his body and propped himself into a semi-upright position on the lawn.

It wasn't easy. The world around him alternated between pitch black and a fragmented cacophony of colors that swirled around his aching head. He didn't know which he disliked more, the colors or the darkness. All he knew was that both made him incredibly dizzy.

Gingerly, he touched his fingers to his forehead and felt something thick and sticky. Dropping his hand back down to eye level, he looked at it and saw blood.

Blood.

Brenda, don't die. Please don't die! Don't leave me here. Please!

The terrified high-pitched voice—his voice—echoed in his brain, taunting him. Reminding him.

Through sheer willpower, Ian managed to block it out.

The way he always did.

Until the next time.

Ian raised his head and looked up at the officer. The man's dark blue shirt was straining against his girth. The third button from the top was about to pop, he noted vaguely.

Ever so slowly, the rest of his surroundings came into focus. And the chain of events that brought him here. Ian remembered the drive through the deserted campus back roads. He'd taken the route on purpose, lucid enough despite his grief and the inebriating mixture in his system, not to want to hurt anyone.

Except for himself.

A surge in his brain had him calling the sudden turn that sent him skidding. And the oncoming tree that had appeared out of nowhere.

He remembered nothing after that.

Dampness penetrated his consciousness as well as his trousers. Dew. What time was it? Three a.m.? Later? He didn't know.

Ian scrubbed his hand over his face and winced as vivid pain swirled through him like a club covered in cacti spines. A thousand points along his body hurt at once.

"You pull me out?" he asked the policeman.

"Not me. You were out when I got here. Maybe you crawled out."

A thin smile touched the policeman's lips. "Looks like some part of you still wants to go on living."

A dry, humorless laugh melded with the night noises around Ian. Nearby there was the sound of something rustling in the ground cover, as if a possum was scurrying away from the scene of the crime.

That's right, run. Run for your life. I'd run with you if I could.

"News to me," Ian muttered. He never wished for life, not for himself. For the others. For them he'd prayed, until he'd realized that the prayers came too late. That they were dead even as he laid there next to them, pinned down and helpless.

Hands splayed on the ground on either side of him, Ian attempted to push himself up to his feet. Every bone in his body screamed in protest, telling him to lay back down.

"Why don't you just stay put?" It wasn't a suggestion coming from the officer, but an order. "I'm going to call this in and get another squad car on the scene."

Because his limbs were made out of recycled gelatin, Ian remained where he was.

"Reinforcements?" A cynical smile curved his mouth. He never thought of himself as dangerous, although Ryan had once described him that way. But then, his publicist was afraid of his own shadow. "Why? I promise not to resist arrest." He couldn't even if he wanted to, Ian thought.

"You sound pretty coherent for a drunk," Officer Holtz commented.

"Practice," Ian replied. In truth, there were more pills in him than alcohol, and maybe he was a little dangerous. Reckless even. Most nights— because nights were when it was the hardest—he could keep a lid on it, could go on. But tonight the pain had won and all he wanted to do was still it. Make it stop.

But it was still there. The physical pain would go away. This never did, no matter what face he showed to the world.

There was a street lamp not too far away and Ian could make out the officer more clearly now. His face was redder than it had been a moment ago.

"Think you're immortal?" the officer jeered.

"I'm really hoping not." His voice was so calm, Ian could see that he had rattled the man.

"Wipe that damn smile off your face," Officer Holtz ordered. "Calling this in is procedure."

Ian gave up attempting to stand. He needed to wait until his limbs could support him. Or maybe until his head stopped bleeding.

Very gingerly, Ian laid back on the damp grass, his head spinning madly like a top off its axis. Oblivion poked long, scratchy black fingers out of the darkness to grab hold of him.

Ian laughed shortly. "Wouldn't want to mess with procedure."

It was the last thing he said before the abyss swallowed him up.

"What the hell were you thinking?"

Marcus Wyman's question reverberated about the small, clean square room within the police station where lawyers were allowed to talk to their clients in private. Anger swelled in his voice and glowed in his small, brown eyes as he regarded his client and friend.

Ten feet away, on the other side of the door, a guard stood at the ready, waiting for the minutes of their allotted time to be over.

Ian leaned back in his chair, tottering slightly on the two back legs. He sat on the far end of the rectangular table. His face was turned from his lawyer as he stared out the window.

That side of the building overlooked a large parking lot that was landscaped with ficus trees that some gardener had shaped like beach umbrellas, an example of city life attempting to appear rustic. City life would win out in the end.

The bad always ate the good, Ian mused, detached.

When he finally responded to Marcus, he sounded oddly hollow. "As a matter of fact, I was trying not to think."

Marcus was a short, stocky man with the nervous habit of massaging his chest, moved restlessly around a room. The man knit his thoughts together in a slow, plodding fashion until they emerged into a complete, meticulously constructed whole. He claimed his nervous habit helped him think. Graying at the temples, his mouth lost in a perpetual frown, it was sometimes hard for people to believe that he was only a year older than Ian.

Having Ian for a friend, he claimed, had aged him.

They'd known each other for close to twenty years, since Ian was eleven, and Marcus liked to think of himself as Ian's one true friend, even though, any so-called in-depth article would claim that Ian Malone—otherwise known as B. D. Brendan, the bestselling author of fifteen science-fiction novels—had a squadron of friends.

Hangers-on were all they were and Ian knew it. His dark good looks, bad-boy reputation and razor-sharp wit lured people, especially women, by the legions. Ian attracted crowds wherever he went. But within his dark, somber soul, Ian Malone was very much alone. Deliberately so.

His friend, Marcus knew, was punishing himself. Punishing himself for something he'd had no control over, no hand in planning. Fate had spared him while taking his parents and his older sister in a devastating earthquake two decades ago. And he never forgave himself for surviving, never stopped asking why he wound up being the one to live while they had died.

Knowing all that, there were still times when Marcus wanted to take the much taller Ian by the shoulders and shake him until he came around. This afternoon was one of those times.

He'd been unceremoniously woken out of a deep sleep at five this morning. Ian, calling from the city jail. He'd been on the case since six.

Ignoring Ian's reply, he went on to make his point. "I had to pull a lot of strings, but I think I've managed to keep this out of the newspapers."

He was talking to the back of Ian's head and it annoyed him. Worried about Ian, he'd snapped at his wife as he hurried out of the house and had skipped breakfast entirely. Neither of which put him in a very good mood.

Receiving no response, no sign that he'd even been heard, Marcus raised his voice. "And I think I can get the standard sentence commuted." Even first-time offenses for DUIs were strict. The courts had made it known that this wasn't something to be viewed lightly. Licenses were immediately suspended, stiff fines and penalties imposed. Not to mention the threat of jail time. "Ian, are you even listening to me?" he asked impatiently.

Ian had heard every word. He remained exactly where he was, staring out the window. "Do you know what yesterday was, Marc?"

Marcus sighed and moved his hand over the ever-widening expanse of his head. Up until four years ago, his hair was as black and as thick as Ian's. But then nature decided to take back what it had so generously given and now there was only a fringe around his ears to mark where his hair had once been.

"The day you wrecked your Porsche?" Marcus guessed wearily.

"No." Ian paused, as if it physically hurt to utter the words. "It was the twenty-first anniversary."

Marcus stiffened.

"I forgot," Marcus admitted, his voice small, apologetic. Had he remembered, and knowing what his friend could be capable of, he would have spent the day with Ian.

Ian exhaled. The small huff of warm breath clouded the window pane. "I didn't."

Crossing to him, Marcus placed his hand on Ian's shoulder. Despite his girth, Marcus was a gentle man and compassion was his hallmark. His wife referred to him as a giant teddy bear. He was the only one, outside of Ian's grandparents, who knew the story. Even so, Marcus always suspected that there was more to it, that Ian had kept back a piece of his grief to torture himself with.

"Ian," Marcus began softly, "you have to let it go sometime. Don't you think that twenty-one years is long enough to wear a hair shirt?"

There was an anger raging within him, but Ian kept it tightly wrapped. Marcus didn't deserve to be lashed out at. He meant well and only tried to help. But Marcus didn't understand what it was like. What it meant to be buried alive, to have the people you loved dead all around you.

Ian moved his shoulder so that Marcus was forced to drop his hand. As he did, he could feel Ian's smoky-blue eyes boring into him.

"No," Ian replied. The word was uttered softly, but there was no missing the underlying passion beneath the word.

Marcus suppressed a sigh. Returning to his end of the table, he slowly ran his hands over the sides of the expensive briefcase Ian had given him when he'd passed his bar exam. At the time, Ian had scarcely been able to afford to pay rent on his run-down studio apartment. But by hocking the gold watch his grandfather had given him, Ian had gotten the money together to buy him the camel-colored leather briefcase. Whenever he lost his temper with Ian, Marcus always looked at the briefcase.

And cooled off.

"Look, this is your first offense, thank God—" Quitting while he was ahead, Marcus didn't ask if there had been other times, times when his friend managed to avoid detection. What he didn't know wouldn't keep him up at night.

"There's a reason for that," Ian said.

He'd never driven under the influence before. When the need to blot out the world overwhelmed him, he'd always drowned his grief at home, alone. Away from prying eyes. Last night represented a crack in his control. And he didn't like it.

Marcus didn't wait for him to elaborate. "I think things can be worked out." He wanted to suggest rehab or a psychiatrist. Neither suggestion would fly with Ian because Ian couldn't admit to the world that there was a weakness underneath his armor. "We've drawn a reasonable judge. The Honorable Sally Houghton. Word is that she has a strong mothering instinct. Just straighten up, look contrite and remember to flash that thousand-watt smile of yours." He snapped his briefcase closed again. "It appears as if your guardian angel is still looking out for you."

Ian chuckled. He could do without guardian angels who saw fit to prolong his suffering. "Yeah."

The word was uttered entirely without feeling.

Then, to Marcus's overwhelming relief, Ian turned around from the window and gave him just the barest of smiles. The one Marcus knew could melt stones at fifty paces and hard-hearted female judges' hearts at ten. And Houghton was a softy. That gave them a definite edge and more than a fighting chance. Ian had a magnetic personality when he wasn't sparring with the ghosts from his past.

Maybe this whole incident was even to the good. Ian might finally put this behind him and get on with the business of living.

And maybe, Marcus thought as he signaled for the guard to unlock the door, while he had been in here talking to Ian, pigs had actually learned how to fly.

Chapter Two

There were times when Lisa Kittridge wondered what she was doing here. And why for the last eighteen months she continued to return to Providence Shelter, week after week, when she really didn't have to. At least, not because of some court order, the way so many others who passed through here did.

God knew it wasn't because time hung heavily on her hands. Absolutely every moment of her day was accounted for, what with thirty-one energetic third graders to teach and a five-year-old and a mother to care for.

Not that Susan Kittridge actually needed looking

after, despite the bullet to the hip that had taken her off the police force and brought a cane into her life. Her mother was one of the most independent women Lisa knew. But every so often, Susan's soul would dip into that black place that beckoned everyone, that place that called for surrender and apathy. During those times, Lisa was her mother's cheering section, drawing on the endless supply of optimism that she'd somehow been blessed with.

Optimism that saw her through her own hard times.

Optimism she felt obliged to share here at the homeless shelter, to pay back a little for the personal happiness she had in her own life. Working at the shelter also accomplished something else. It made her too busy to think about Matt. Very much.

But then, there were days like today, when her cheerfulness seemed to go down several levels. She worked harder then. Longer.

Her work wasn't excessively difficult. Not that she minded hard work. She thrived on it, her late father liked to boast. And if all that was required of her to help out here was a strong back and endless energy, then working at the shelter would have been a piece of cake.

But it wasn't all. There was more. A great deal more.

Every so often, the hurt she found herself facing grew to such proportions that it became too much for her to endure emotionally. Looking into the faces of the children sometimes tore at her heart so badly she didn't think she could recover, certainly not enough to come back.

But she always did.

She'd initially volunteered at Providence Shelter in order to make a difference in these people's lives. Instead, the people she interacted with had made a difference in hers. They made her humbler. More grateful. And more determined than ever to help.

Help people such as the little girl on the cot.

Lisa had walked into the long, communal sleeping area with an armload of fresh bedding that needed to be distributed. She saw the girl immediately—there was no one else in the room and the little girl was a new face. A new, frightened face.

She was sitting on the cot, her thin arms braced on either side of her equally thin body, dangling her spindly legs as if that were her only source of entertainment, the only thing she had any command over.

As Lisa came closer, the little girl looked up suddenly, suspicion and fear leaping into her wide, gray eyes.

Oh God, no child should have to look like that, Lisa thought. Her son was around this girl's age.

The mother in her ached for the little girl. For all the little girls and boys who'd found themselves within the walls of homeless shelters because of some cruel twist of fate.

Very carefully, Lisa laid down the bedding she was holding and smiled at the little girl. "Hi, what's your name?"

The wide eyes continued to stare at her. There was no answer.

Lisa sat down on one edge of the cot. The girl quickly moved to the opposite corner, like a field mouse frightened away by the vibration of footsteps.

"You don't talk to strangers," Lisa guessed. The little girl nodded solemnly, never taking her eyes away. "That's very good. You shouldn't. I've got a little boy just your age and that's what I tell him, too." She smiled warmly at the child. "My name is Lisa," she told her. "I'm a volunteer here." Lisa extended her hand toward the small fingers that were clutched together in the little girl's lap. "I help out here at Providence when I can."

Lisa had an overwhelming desire to wash away the smudges on the small, thin face and brush the tangles out of the thick, brown hair. But first she had to win the girl's trust and, depending on what the child had been through and what she had seen, that might not be very easy.

"If you need anything," she told the girl, "just ask me."

The small hands remained clasped together.

Lisa rose to her feet. She didn't want the child to feel crowded or pressured in any way. "Remember, if you need anything, my name's Lisa."

Picking up the bedding, she began to distribute the folded, freshly laundered sheets. She'd just placed the last one down when she heard a small voice behind her say, "Daddy."

Lisa turned around, not completely certain whether she'd actually heard the word or imagined it. "Did you say something, honey?"

"Daddy," the girl whispered again in the same soft, timid voice.

Lisa's mind raced. Either the little girl was telling her that she was afraid of her father—so many women and children here had been abused—or that she wanted her father. She couldn't tell by the girl's expression, which had not changed. Lisa took a chance and focused on the fact that she had used the word "need" when she'd spoken to the little girl.

"Do you want me to find your daddy for you?"

The dark head bobbed up and down. "Yes."

Was the man here somewhere at the shelter? Or had he abandoned his family before they ever found their way to this place? She needed more input, but right now, there was no one else to ask for details. "Can you tell me what your daddy looks like, honey?"

Before the little girl could answer, a tall, thin woman with premature lines etched into her face entered the room. She looked relieved to see the little girl sitting there. And then she looked angry.

Crossing to her, the woman wrapped her arms protectively around the child's shoulders and pulled her to her feet. She pressed the girl to her, as if to absorb her. Or at the very least, keep her out of harm's way.

"There's no sense in you looking for him," the woman snapped at Lisa. Her anger at the invasion, at being stripped of everything, even pride, pulsated in the air between them like barely harnessed electricity. "Monica's daddy left us almost two years ago. Couldn't stand watching us do without anymore. Like leaving helped." Bitterness twisted the woman's pinched mouth. "He's the reason we're here. Monica thinks he'll come back even though I keep telling her he won't."

Lisa knew all about hanging on emotionally even when logic dictated otherwise. "Everyone needs to be able to hope," she said, gently touching the little girl's cheek.

"What everyone needs is to be prepared for disappointment," a deep male voice rumbled behind her.

There was no malice in the voice, no overwhelming cynicism. Only resignation to the facts.

Swinging around, Lisa found herself looking up at a tall, darkly handsome man with intense ice-blue eyes. The sensual smile never reached his eyes or any other part of him.

She'd never seen him before.

He was dressed casually, but the dark-blue pullover and gray slacks looked expensive. The man seemed as out of place here as a genuine pearl necklace in a drawer full of costume jewelry.

Here comes trouble.

She had no idea where the thought had come from, but it flashed across her mind the second she saw him. The second his eyes touched hers.

"Who are you?"

Her voice sounded a little sharp to her own ear, but she didn't like his philosophy. Liked even less that he expressed it in front of a child.

Behind her, she heard Monica and her mother leaving the room. She made a mental note to bring a small doll with her for Monica the next time she came.

If Monica was still here. Every little girl deserved to have a doll.

She looked at the stranger, still waiting for an answer. Was this some kind of a game for him? She was aware of his scrutiny. As if she was someone he needed to evaluate before answering. Just who did he think he was?

"Well?" she asked.

She had a temper, Ian thought. Probably helped her survive what she had to deal with in a place like this. "Ian Malone, at your service."

He waited a moment to see if there was a glimmer of recognition. He didn't write under his own name, but it wasn't exactly a state secret that Ian Malone and B. D. Brendan were one and the same.

But there was nothing in the woman's face to indicate that the name—or he—meant anything at all to her. *Good.* Even though writing was the only lifeline that he still clung to—and even that had been failing him for the past nine months—there were times when fame got on his nerves. It made him want to shed his skin, a snake ready to move on to the next layer.

She wasn't saying anything, so he added, "I was told to report to you for instructions." Marcus had dropped him off here, promising to be by later to pick him up. Marcus had made it seem like a feather in his cap, getting him this community service gig. Looking around, he was beginning to think a little jail time wouldn't have been such a bad thing. "You are Lisa Kittridge, right?"

"Right," she fired back at him. She didn't like his attitude, she didn't like him. One of the privileged who'd come here, slumming, to atone for a social transgression. She'd seen his kind before. "Who told you to *report* to me?"

"A little bird-like woman at the front desk." He turned in that general direction. "British accent, bad taste in clothes."

"That would be Muriel." She took offense for the other woman. Muriel ran the shelter and had a heart as large as Dodger Stadium. "And for your information, I think she dresses rather well."

"Can't help that," he murmured under his breath, then asked, "Is she a friend of yours?"

He asked a hell of a lot of questions for someone who'd been sent here in lieu of jail time, she thought. She felt her back going up even more. "We don't go on retreats together or braid each other's hair, but yes, you could say we're friends."

"Then I'd clue her in if I were you. Better yet," his eyes washed over her and there was a glint of appreciation in them, "you could take her shopping with you the next time you go."

She wasn't flattered. She was annoyed. "Is this an effort for you, or does being obnoxious just come naturally?"

The smile gave no sign of fading. If anything, he looked even more amused. "It's a gift," he told her dryly.

"One you should return," she countered. Because she was short of funds and long on work, Muriel had gotten to the point where she relied on Lisa heavily, so Lisa knew she had to make the best of this conceited misfit they'd been sent for however long he was here. "Let me guess, community service, right?"

Ian inclined his head, giving her the point. "The lady gets a prize."

The shelter saw its share of first-time offenders whose sentences were commuted to volunteering a number of hours working for either the city or a charitable organization. Most of the time, the men and women came, did what was required of them and left without any fanfare, wanting to get it over with as quickly, as quietly as possible.

This one was different. This one had an attitude. Terrific.

"And just what was it that they found you guilty of?" she asked.

The answer came without any need for thought. "Living."

"If that were the case, the shelter would never be shorthanded. What did the judge say you did?" she pressed. The sooner she got him to admit accountability, the more readily he would move on. Or, at least she hoped so.

He shrugged carelessly. He'd never liked giving an account of himself. It reminded him too much of being grilled by his grandfather. "My car had a difference of opinion with a tree. They both wanted to occupy the same place. The tree won."

Her eyes swept over him. There were no signs that he'd even been in an accident. He had one small scar over his left eye, but that had long since healed and grown faint with time, so she doubted that he'd sustained it in an accident. "You don't look any the worse for it."

His mouth twisted in a semi-smile. "Too bad my car can't say the same thing."

Her eyes darkened like a sudden storm sweeping over the horizon. "You were drunk."

He watched, fascinated by the transformation. She looked as if she would have thought nothing of grinding him into the ground. "Kitty, what I was—and am—is my business."

"Lisa," she corrected coldly. "My name is Lisa. Or, in your case, Miss Kittridge. And since you're here, you've become my business."

The smile was warm, disarming. It startled her how quickly it all but filleted her clear down to the bone. "Sounds promising."

Lisa mentally rolled up her sleeves. "Okay, Malone, the first thing you're going to have to understand is that this isn't a game and that you're not slumming. After your time here, you get to go home at the end of the day. For most of these people, this *is* home. You will treat it—and them—with respect and do what you can to make the experience of being here less painful for them."

She was almost barking out the orders. "You a drill sergeant in your spare time?"

Her eyes narrowed again. Damn, but they were scraping the bottom of the barrel with this one. "No, a human being."

"Ouch."

She didn't return his smile. She meant to get a fair amount of real work out of him. The shelter was always in need of some sort of repair. The boiler didn't sound as if it was going to make it through another winter and there were holes in the roof the size of well-fed rats. The rainy season was just around the corner, right after Thanksgiving. That didn't give them much time to get into shape.

Lisa glanced down at his shoes. "Your Italian loafers are going to get dirty here."

Their eyes met as she looked up again. She found his smile really unsettling. "You know quality."

Lisa looked at him pointedly. "Yes, I do." The way she said it, her meaning was clear.

Ian laughed. Most of the time he dealt with people who fawned over him. People who wouldn't know an honest emotion if it bit them.

She, obviously, did not fall into that category. "I like you, Kitty."

She started to correct him again, then decided it wasn't worth it. Maybe if she just ignored his attempt at familiarity, the man would eventually give it up. He didn't look as if he had much of an attention span. "How are you with a hammer?"

He'd built his own sailboat once. Actually, he and Marcus had. Marcus had talked him into it the summer before they graduated college. Marcus from Yale, he from NYU. But this woman looked like she'd probably consider that bragging, so instead, he shrugged. "I know which end to use."

She sighed. Not handy, either. This was just getting better and better. "It's a start," she allowed.

"That it is," he responded.

Ignoring the comment, or the chipper way he delivered it, she made a quick assessment of his body. He was muscular and lean, although she doubted he'd actually ever done any physical labor. He didn't seem the type. Too bad, but he'd learn.

She thought of the most pressing repair item on her list. "Do heights bother you?"

His eyes slid over her body. She had the impression of being weighed and measured. It surprised her that there was a part of her that wondered, just for a moment, what his conclusions were.

"That depends on what I'm doing," he finally answered.

Why did she feel as if she'd just been propositioned? "Nailing shingles," she bit off.

His smile just widened. And burrowed into her despite her resistance. "Any chance of that being a euphemism?"

"None whatsoever," she replied evenly.

"Didn't think so." It would feel good to do something physical for a change, he thought. Something to work up a sweat. "I can give it a try."

"You need to do more than 'try,'" she informed him, barely hanging onto her patience.

This wasn't going to work, she thought, not with the attitude she saw. Granted she didn't draw a salary here and her time was limited, but she felt part of something at Providence, something that went beyond a paycheck. And these people deserved better than having some bored blight on society doing halfhearted penance because he'd gotten caught going too fast after parking his judgment.

"Look, Malone, you either take this job seriously or have your hotshot lawyer get you reassigned to something else."

The term made him laugh. If there was *anything* that Marcus wasn't, it was a hotshot. "Marcus would really get insulted by that last remark."

"Marcus?" Who the hell was Marcus? Or was he just trying to distract her?

"My lawyer. My friend," he added. "He's really a very dedicated person." Ian's mouth curved. "Not like me at all."

She'd heard his voice soften, just for a moment, when he'd mentioned the man. Maybe this Marcus he mentioned really was a friend. If so, that meant that he was capable of maintaining a relationship with something other than his own photograph. Maybe there was hope for him.

Maybe all this was just bravado because being around the homeless and downtrodden made him nervous. It wouldn't be the first time that had happened.

"He's as solid as a brick wall," Ian continued. "And he's as far from a *hotshot* as you are from possessing a sense of humor."

He'd had her going there for a minute, thinking that maybe she'd been too hard on him. First impressions were usually right. And her first impression of him—good looks or no good looks—was far from favorable.

Ian watched in fascination as he saw her eyes flash. They turned from a light green to something he had once seen during a squall. He had a feeling that when she really got going, she was something else. The part of him that dissected and explored, that looked inside of every word, every sensation, every feeling, experienced a curiosity to discover what the woman before him was like when all of her buttons were pressed.

"I don't laugh very much here, Mr. Malone."

The retort just came out. It was, in actuality, a lie. Whenever possible, she tried very hard to bring laughter into these people's lives. If not laughter, then at least a smile. But somehow, with Malone, that laughter seemed synonymous with a joke. And there were precious few jokes here.

"I don't suggest you do, either," she added. Lisa drew herself up, painfully aware that she was at least a foot shorter than this annoying man. It made her feel as if she were at a severe disadvantage and she didn't like that. "Now if you're through making observations, I'll take you to that hammer."

She turned on her heel and began to walk quickly from the room. Taking a second to admire the view from where he was, the way her hips subtly moved with each step, Ian fell into step with her. Because of his longer stride, he caught up within a moment.

"Looking forward to it," he told her.

And she was looking forward to his hours of community service being over, she thought. Absently, she wondered just how many hours he owed the city. At the same time, she thanked God that she wouldn't have to be here for most of them.

Chapter Three

Lisa glanced at her watch. It was almost seven. She'd stayed longer than she'd intended. Again. Whenever she came to Providence Shelter, time melted into this distant dimension and she lost all sense of it. One thing led to another and she would never seem to finish. But that was life. Ongoing. Neverending.

But right now her life was waiting for her back at her house and if she didn't hurry, she was going to miss reading Casey his bedtime story. He was pretty out of sorts with her over the last time she'd come home late, only to find him fast asleep. She'd had to bribe him by letting him stay up an extra half hour on Friday night in order to get him to forgive her. She didn't want that to become a habit.

Not to mention she still had papers that needed to be graded. She really owed it to her students not to fall asleep over them the way she had last time.

That's what she got by trying to make do on five hours sleep, she silently upbraided herself. As her mother had pointed out to her more than once, she wasn't a superwoman. There was no point in trying to act like one.

Just before she left, Lisa swung by Muriel's office to get her purse. The room was empty. Just as well, Lisa decided. She didn't want to get caught up in a conversation at this hour. Muriel was a lovely person, but she could go on indefinitely without ever reaching her point.

Crossing to the old desk someone had donated to the building, she opened the bottom drawer and took out her purse. Lisa closed the drawer and slung the purse strap onto her shoulder. She was ready to leave.

But she didn't.

Whether it was a sense of responsibility or just plain old-fashioned curiosity, she couldn't honestly say, but instead of leaving the building, Lisa found herself retracing her steps and going outside, where less than two hours ago, she'd left Providence Shelter's latest penitent perched on a ladder, ready to make the necessary interim repairs to the roof.

Or so he had said.

Closing the door behind her, she looked around the back. Part of her expected to find Malone sprawled out on the ground, unconscious, a victim of a sudden attack of vertigo or some such paltry excuse.

Granted she might have been a tad too hard on him, but something about him reminded her of the last man she'd had the misfortune of dating. Thad, the divorced father of one of her students, had been charming on the outside, hollow in the inside. In the end, she honestly didn't know who she was more disappointed in, him for stepping out on her or herself for being such a poor judge of character.

She knew better now.

Apparently not, Lisa silently amended the next moment as she circled around to the rear of the building and found the ladder just where she'd left it. Malone was definitely not where she had left him. Not on the ladder, not anywhere in sight.

Lisa could feel her jaw tighten. The man had fled the coop. Already. Blowing out a breath, she swallowed an oath. She might have known.

It was obvious that Malone couldn't stick to a commitment. But she would have thought he'd at least last out the day. Frowning, she went back inside to see if she could find one of the older boys to move the ladder and put it away. It obviously couldn't stay where it was. Thanks to Casey and her teaching position, she was well acquainted with the way the minds of the under-four-foot set worked. The ladder and all it represented was far too much of a temptation for the smaller residents of Providence Shelter.

As she turned the corner, she nearly bumped into Muriel. Lost in thought, the older woman was humming to herself. Lisa couldn't remember *ever* seeing the woman look anything but sunny and optimistic.

"Leaving, dear?" Muriel asked.

Lisa nodded. "I've got to be getting home." She hesitated for a second, debating saying anything. Technically, it wasn't any of her business. But she had never operated that way, keeping out of her fellow man or woman's business. Doing so would have made the world a very cold, isolated place as far as she was concerned.

Besides, Muriel deserved to know. She was far too busy to be aware of every little detail that went on at the house.

"Look, that new guy, the one the court sent here because of a DUI," even saying the acronym constricted her throat. "I really don't think that he's going to work out."

The look on the woman's face told Lisa that Muriel knew instantly who she was referring to. "You mean the one who makes me wish I were twenty years younger?" The wistful smile on Muriel's lips was unmistakable. "What makes you say that?"

Muriel was the kind who would find redeeming qualities in Genghis Khan, Lisa thought. "Well, I told him to replace the shingles that flew off the roof in that storm we had last month."

"Good, good." Muriel nodded, then seemed to realize that there was obviously more. "And?"

Lisa spread her hands wide. "And I just looked and he's not there."

Muriel glanced out the back window automatically, even though there was no way she could see the area under discussion. In addition, twilight had long since sneaked its way across the terrain.

"When did you tell him to do it?"

Lisa thought for a moment, trying to remember the time. "A little less than a couple of hours ago."

Muriel's expression all but said, *Well, there you have it,* but she added audibly, "Maybe he's finished."

Lisa didn't have to get on the ladder to know the answer to that one. An expert might have completed the job, but Malone was no expert. "I doubt it. He's not the handy type."

The smile on Muriel's lips turned positively wicked as it reached her eyes and made them sparkle. "That probably all depends on what you mean by handy." The smile widened as Muriel's thoughts took flight. "He strikes me as someone who could be *very* handy under the right circumstances."

Lisa could only shake her head. Muriel spent

most of her time here. It was obvious that she needed to get out and socialize more. "Muriel, you've been a widow too long."

The woman's dark brown eyes met hers. "You should talk."

This wasn't about her. Not in any manner, shape or form. "I'm not a widow," Lisa reminded the other woman. "Casey's father and I never got the chance to get married."

Not that there hadn't been plans, lots of plans. Plans that never had a chance to become a reality because the weekend before the wedding, Matt was struck by a drunk driver. He'd died instantly at the scene.

It had taken her a long time to recover and make her peace with what had happened. Having Casey in her life had helped most of all. But even that caused her to ache a little in the middle of the night. Ache because she had never gotten the chance to tell Matt that she was pregnant. He'd died without ever knowing that they had created a son.

"You know," Muriel began slowly, running the tip of her tongue along her bright-red lips, "this Ian fellow might—"

"Stop right there," Lisa warned abruptly, raising her hand like a traffic cop. "You have the same glint in your eyes that my mother periodically gets." The one that would come into her mother's eyes when she'd talk about friends' unattached sons or nephews who just happened to be in town for the week. "And

I can tell you right here, right now, that not even if Ian Malone were the last man on earth and tipped in gold would I entertain the idea of hooking my wagon to his star."

"Interesting way of putting it," a male voice interrupted.

Caught, Lisa could only look at Muriel's face. The older woman didn't bother suppressing her grin as she nodded her head. Malone. Somehow or other, the man had managed to sneak up behind her.

Okay, this wasn't the time to look guilty. Instead, she summoned the indignation she'd felt when she'd first happened upon the unattended ladder.

Swinging around, Lisa went on the offensive. Her late father, a football coach for a semipro team, had always been a big believer in using offense rather than defense.

"I thought you went home."

Ian summoned an innocent expression, enjoying himself. "My time wasn't up yet."

He might fool Muriel, but he wasn't fooling her. "Then why didn't you finish putting up the new shingles like I asked you?"

"You didn't ask," he corrected her, "you told. And I did." Before she could open her mouth to challenge his answer, he had a question of his own. "Did you bother looking at the roof?"

She seemed annoyed, which gave him his answer. "From the ground," Lisa said grudgingly.

He infuriated her by shaking his head. "Can't see the new shingles from that angle."

Ian found the suspicion that clouded her eyes oddly attractive. There was chemistry here, he noted, wondering if she was aware of it. Probably the reason she was snapping his head off.

"So you finished."

Ian inclined his head and then saluted smartly. "Yes, ma'am, I did indeed."

She'd believe it when she saw it, Lisa thought, but for now, she let that argument go. "So where were you?"

"I was in the activity room." He nodded in the general direction of the room he had just vacated. It was also known as the common room and was where everyone gathered in the latter part of the day. "I didn't realize that I had to ask anyone for permission before I walked anywhere."

"You don't," she shot back, feeling like a shrew even as she went on talking. Muriel, she noticed, seemed content just to stand by the wayside and observe. "But there were other things you could have been helping with."

"I know," he said. His eyes shifted toward Muriel and he smiled. "I was."

Muriel was too softhearted for her own good and she wasn't about to stand around and watch her being manipulated. So she became the other woman's champion and challenged Malone. "Like what?"

"I read a story," he said simply.

Did he think he could just sit back and relax because he happened to be better looking than most movie stars? That didn't give him a get-out-of-jail-free card. Not in her book.

"You can read on your own time, Mr. Malone," Lisa informed him. "The court didn't send you here to entertain yourself."

"I wasn't," he contradicted. "I was entertaining your little friend."

Lisa narrowed her eyes. She hadn't the slightest idea what this man was talking about. "What little friend?"

"The little girl you were trying to bolster when I found you earlier." It took him a second to remember the name the girl's mother had used. "Monica. She looked lonely when I walked by, I stopped and gave her a book." A whole stack of worn children's books sat on one of the tables. The girl had looked embarrassed and had just held the thin book. That was when his suspicions had been aroused. "Except that somewhere along the line, public education failed her because she can't read." As quickly as his anger rose, it abated, hiding behind the shield he always had fixed in place. "So I read to her." He looked at her intently and directed his question to Lisa rather than the woman who was paid to run the shelter. "Or is that against the rules?"

Lisa shifted, feeling uncomfortable. What's more,

she felt like an idiot. Maybe she was being too hard on Malone. After all, she didn't really know him. His attitude just rubbed her the wrong way and had led her to certain conclusions.

To *jump* to certain conclusions, she amended, chagrinned.

"No," she said, "that's not against the rules." Lisa paused, pressing her lips together. "I guess I owe you an apology."

There was amusement in the blue eyes. They weren't icy, she decided, changing her initial opinion. They were warm. Maybe a little *too* warm.

"It might sound more convincing if you didn't act as if your mouth were filled with unappetizing dirt when you said it."

"As opposed to the appetizing kind?" she guessed.

Ian laughed. She'd gotten him. Words were his stock and trade, but of late, in the last nine months, it felt as if he'd just closed up shop. Nothing was coming. No ideas, no snippets of plots, no stray dialogue flashing through his brain at odd moments, begging to be written down before they were forgotten. It was as if his fictional world, the world he often sought out for solace and in which he often took refuge, had completely deserted him, leaving him to fend for himself and deal with what was around him without the crutch he had come to rely on so heavily.

This with a deadline breathing down his neck.

For now, he smiled, his eyes on hers. "I stand corrected," he allowed.

He looked over Lisa's head at the woman he had checked in with when he'd first walked through the doors. He couldn't help wondering if she was very shrewd or very vacant. Her expression could be read either way.

"Has anyone thought about setting up a few informal classes to teach the kids while they're staying here? If most of them are transient, then enrolling in the local schools doesn't sound like anything their parents are going to be looking into. Whole chunks of these kids' educations are falling through the cracks and nobody's noticing."

Lisa looked at him, surprised by the observation. *Was* he actually deeper than that brilliantly blinding smile of his? "You sound like you've given this matter some thought." She studied him for a moment, looking to be swayed one way or the other about him. "Like you're familiar with it."

The shrug was careless, tying him to nothing. "In a manner of speaking."

Given the glimmer of a hint, Lisa wasn't about to back off easily. "What manner of speaking?"

"Mine," he replied.

The single word just hung there, suspended in space. Ian didn't feel like sharing anymore, didn't feel like telling this woman or her superior that he'd once been one of those kids who'd had sections of his life carelessly lost in the shuffle because no one was looking out for him.

After his family had been killed in the Palm Springs earthquake, it had taken Social Services more than six months to locate his mother's parents. His grandparents, Ed and Louise Humboldt, lived on a small operating farm in Northern California, close to the Oregon border. Estranged from their daughter because of her marriage to a man they didn't feel was good enough for her, they had no idea that anything had happened to her or to her husband and daughter, until Alice McKay from the Orange Country Social Services office had taken it upon herself, on her own time, to locate his only living relatives.

They were little more than strangers to him when Alice brought him up to the farm. He hadn't wanted to stay with them, had wanted instead to go home with Alice because she was kind and her smile reminded him of his sister's. But that wasn't possible. So he had remained with his grandparents, who took him in out of a sense of duty.

They fed him, clothed him and gave him a roof over his head. In exchange, he did chores on the farm before school, after school and practically until he dropped at night.

Ed and Louise were good people, they just weren't good grandparents. He knew they didn't love him. They didn't concern themselves with his education other than his getting one. He thought of running away several times, but instead, he remained. And then, as he settled in, a funny thing happened.

A whole new world opened up for him whenever he was around books. A world where there was no weight on his shoulders, no pain waiting for him around every corner and no guilt ready to spring up at him without warning. He read everything he could get his hands on, especially science fiction.

When he wasn't doing chores or studying for school, he was reading. Morning, noon and night.

Around the time when he turned fifteen, he discovered that he could not only read about those worlds that existed between the pages of a book, he could create them. Create worlds where things happened the way he wanted them to. He wasn't a victim anymore. Instead, he became a god. A god who presided over invisible worlds that existed first only in his mind and then on paper as well.

He finished writing his first book at seventeen, fashioning a strange world where people were ruled by their nightmares. Twenty-seven publishers rejected it. And one made him an offer.

He was on his way.

None of it would have happened if Alice McKay hadn't taken it upon herself to hunt down his mother's parents. Because if she hadn't, if she had been content to do her job and nothing more, he would have gone on being sent from one foster home to another, one school system to another and, because of his progressively rebellious nature, never remaining anywhere long enough to learn anything or find any peace.

He'd dedicated *Nightmares* to her, paying her the highest compliment that he could by making her the godmother of his firstborn.

"I think it's a good idea," Muriel decided, after thinking about the idea of classes for a moment. Her eyes shifted back and forth between the two of them, finally resting on Lisa. "Why don't the two of you see what can be worked out?"

Lisa frowned. She didn't want to be pulled into this. Redeeming idea or not, she didn't like the thought of working too closely with Malone. One altruistic moment did not a saint make.

"It's his idea," she protested, looking at Muriel pointedly.

The expression on Muriel's face was mild. But once she'd made up her mind, nothing could dissuade it. "Yes, but you're the teacher," she reminded her.

That shouldn't be held against her, Lisa thought, irritated.

Ian looked at her with mild surprise. "You're a teacher?"

Lisa unconsciously squared her shoulders. "Yes." She braced herself for some sort of crack. She wasn't disappointed.

His mouth curved slowly, lazily. Wickedly. "No wonder I kept having the strange sensation of having my knuckles rapped."

"Very funny." She looked at him pointedly and decided—again—that she didn't like his attitude. "If I were to rap something, it wouldn't be your knuckles."

He didn't back off. She hadn't thought he would. "Tell me more, this is getting to sound interesting."

Lisa caught herself growing angrier without being entirely sure why. "Is everything a joke to you?"

"If you don't laugh, you cry," he told her with more solemnity than she thought possible.

And then that engaging grin of his took over, turning everything in its path to jelly. Or worse.

He glanced over her head through the window and his expression changed. It made her think of a prisoner who had just seen his parole papers placed on the warden's desk. "Looks like my ride's here."

"Your ride?" she echoed, turning around to see for herself. She saw a light-blue Corvette pull up right before the front steps.

He nodded, rolling down his sleeves and buttoning them at his wrist.

"The state of California doesn't want me driving around right now. Something about people not being safe on the streets. See you, Kitty. We'll talk more next time." And then he winked at her just before he left the premises.

She tried not to notice that something in her stomach fluttered in response.

Chapter Four

"I know, I know," Lisa called out even before she made it across the threshold, her key still in the lock. Removing the key and closing the door behind her, she dropped her purse beneath the coatrack and kicked off her shoes, an indication that she was officially home. "I'm late. Sorry."

The words were addressed to her mother who she knew would be somewhere within the vicinity of the front door. Widowed, Susan Kittridge had moved in with her just after a bullet to the hip had terminated her career with the Bedford police force. Unable to remain on the sidelines, her mother had gotten a job with a nationwide security firm, taking the evening shift so that there would always be someone home for Casey.

Lisa flashed her mother an apologetic look. She knew that the woman was due at work soon.

Without missing a beat, Susan crossed to the entrance and picked up both the purse and the shoes. Depositing them in the hall closet, her mother feigned innocence.

"I didn't say anything." Susan closed the closet door firmly.

Lisa gave her mother a knowing look. "But you were thinking it."

Susan laughed softly, shaking her head. "My daughter, the mind reader." Because she didn't really have to leave for another twenty minutes, Susan paused and gave herself a few minutes just to talk. Conversations were rare between them lately. Words were tossed around on the fly as Lisa hurried off in the morning and she at night. "You know, the FBI probably has a great opening for someone with your talent."

Maybe she was feeling edgy, but she took her mother's words as a criticism. She was in no mood to defend herself or get into a verbal battle. "It's been a long day, Mom."

"And this makes it different—how?"

About to retort, Lisa stopped herself. There was no reason to take offense. She knew her mother hadn't intended her question that way. She was just being testy. It was all Malone's fault, she thought. From start to finish.

"You're right. But the shelter got saddled with one of these community service people this afternoon…"

Which meant that *she* got saddled with him, Lisa thought grudgingly, her voice trailing off. After all, Muriel could only do so much and since the funds had been cut, there was no money for a full-time assistant. The powers that be expected Muriel to do it all, or to depend on volunteers and court-ordered penitents doing atoning servitude.

Like Malone.

Ordinarily, she wouldn't even give the community service people a second thought. But Malone had not only gotten a second thought from her, but a third and fourth one as well. The very fact that he kept preying on her mind bothered her more than she could say.

Susan waited. When her daughter didn't say anything further, she coaxed, "Yes?"

Lisa shrugged. "There's just something so irritating about him."

Susan smiled and shook her head. She knew that Lisa sometimes grew impatient with people who weren't as dedicated as she was. She was like that about teaching as well. As much as she loved her daughter sometimes, Lisa took herself too seriously. "You just have to remember that not everyone is as holy as you are."

About to go upstairs to check on her son, Lisa

stopped dead and swung around to look at her mother. That made it sound as if she looked down her nose at everyone and that just wasn't true. "Mom!"

"Well, you try to be," Susan replied matter-of-factly. There was affection in her eyes, as well as concern. "I'm still trying to figure out what you're trying to prove, but then, I was never very good at puzzling things like that out. Probably why I never made detective," she added philosophically.

"You didn't make detective because you never studied for the exam. You liked being out on the street too much," Lisa reminded her, then added with a touch of indignation, "And I'm not trying to prove anything—"

Now here they had a difference of opinion and of the two of them, Susan thought, she was the one who had the clearer picture.

"Other than the fact that you're superwoman disguised as the not-so-mild-mannered Lisa Kittridge?" Before Lisa could protest, Susan cited the positions on her daughter's unwritten résumé. "Super-mother, super-teacher, super-volunteer. On the daughter front," Susan held out her hand and waffled it a little from side to side, "not so much, but as for the rest of it—"

Lisa sighed, running a hand through her straight black hair. She supposed her mother had a point. She was an overachiever. But then, she always had been.

"So I'm enthusiastic. Is it so wrong to be enthusiastic?"

There was enthusiasm and then there was compulsion. Susan worried that her daughter was leaning toward the latter. She had been ever since Matt had been killed by that drunk driver. "24–7? Yes, it's wrong. Baby, you're burning the candle at both ends."

Susan saw a familiar look slip over Lisa's face. The look that said her stubborn daughter was shutting down. And that no trespassers were welcomed. "My candle, Mother."

"Yes," Susan agreed. "And Casey's," she reminded her quietly.

At the mention of her son's name, Lisa's eyes widened. "Casey. Omigod, Casey." For a moment, she'd forgotten all about him. A wave of guilt washed over her. "Was he very upset when he found out I wasn't going to be home in time to read his story to him before he went to bed?"

Susan allowed herself a smile as she shook her head. "No."

That didn't sound like her Casey, Lisa thought. Was he coming down with something? "No?"

"No," Susan repeated. "Because Casey didn't go to bed."

"He didn't?" Lisa didn't finish as she looked over her shoulder and up the stairs. It was almost eight o'clock. Casey has a seven o'clock bedtime. Occasionally, seven-thirty. "He's still up?"

Susan nodded. She went to the hall closet and retrieved her purse, which looked like a smaller
version of a knapsack but served her purpose well.
"In his room, waiting for you to tell him what
happened to the *Indian in the Cupboard.*"

Lisa sighed. That was the title of the book they
were currently reading each night. Her son could be
very willful when he wanted to be. But she'd thought
that her mother could deal with that, given the
strength of her personality. Obviously she hadn't
factored in the grandmother-pushover component.
"Mom, why didn't you get him into bed?"

"Oh, he's in bed all right." Susan passed the strap
over her head and onto the opposite shoulder, mes-
senger fashion. "Sleeping is another matter. He's his
mother's son," Susan told her daughter pointedly. "As
I recall, I could never make you do anything you
didn't want to do even at that young, tender age,
either."

Lisa didn't bother wasting any more time discuss-
ing who was the adult here. Besides, her mother had
to leave for work. And she had one young man to put
in his place. Taking the stairs two at a time, she raced
up to the small bedroom that was opposite hers.

The door to her son's room was ajar and she
looked in. Casey was sitting in bed, propped up by
the three extra pillows that were up against his head-
board. His eyelids were drooping but they flew open
immediately as the door opened.

When he saw his mother, a smile flashed across his lips, gone the next moment as he struggled to be a miniature adult instead of a five-year-old.

"You're late," he told her in a voice that sounded way too old to please her.

"Yes, I know, and I'm sorry." Crossing to his bed, she turned the lights down a notch, bringing shadows out from the backyard and casting them onto the ceiling. "Couldn't be helped."

"How come you always help all those kids but you forget about me?"

Sitting down on the bed beside her son, Lisa slipped her arm around his shoulders and kissed the top of his head. Casey's hair was straight and the color of newly minted gold. Like his father's had been, she recalled. But Casey's smile, his eyes, his manner, they all belonged to her side of the family. To her.

"I don't forget about you," she insisted in a voice filled with love and patience. "It's just that those kids have nobody and you have me, you have G-Mama, you have Uncle Frank. You have lots of people who love you very much," she emphasized. "The kids I see have next to nothing and no one." She went on stroking Casey's hair. The soft, silky feel was soothing. "I met a little girl today. She's around your age. And she can't read."

"Can't read?" her son echoed, his eyes widening. "What's wrong with her?"

"Nothing's wrong with her," Lisa replied. In the distance, she heard the front door close. Her mother had left for the night. Now it was just Casey and her. "Nobody ever took the time to teach her."

Casey screwed up his face, trying hard to understand. "Doesn't she go to school?"

Everything was so simple at Casey's age. She wished she could keep him this way forever, protect him from a world where disappointments outnumbered triumphs, at times by frightening numbers. But in the long run, she knew it would be doing him a disservice.

So instead, she tightened her arm around him just for a second, loving him as much as she could. "She's homeless, honey. Homeless kids don't always get to go to school like you do."

He nodded, accepting his mother's word. "Are you going to teach her to read, Mommy?"

"Maybe." If Monica wasn't gone by the next time she stopped by the shelter, she added silently.

Before she could say anything else, Casey scrambled out of bed. "Hey, where are you going, cowboy?"

Instead of answering, Casey dropped to his knees in front of the long, double-tiered bookcase that ran along the opposite wall. After finding the book he was looking for, he pulled it free of the others and brought it back to her.

Casey was beaming when he handed the book to her.

Lisa read the title. "*Marvin K. Mooney Will You Please Go Now?*" Surprised, she looked down at her son. Casey was wiggling back into bed, pulling the covers up over himself. "This is the first book you ever read by yourself."

She remembered how he kept asking her to read the popular Dr. Seuss story to him over and over again and how, the first time he read it out loud to her, she was certain he had just memorized the words. He was, after all, barely four. She'd been both surprised and pleased beyond words when he picked words out of context to prove to her that he actually *could* read the book.

Casey nodded. "It's easy," he told her matter-of-factly. "Maybe you can teach her with this."

Overwhelmed, Lisa blinked back tears as she hugged the little boy to her. "You really are a special, special boy, Casey."

Casey tried to wiggle out of her grasp. "Mommy, you're squishing me," he protested, his voice muffled against her side.

"Sorry," she laughed, releasing him. Setting the Dr. Seuss book aside for the moment, she looked at him. "Ready to find out what happened to our friend the indian?" Silken hair bobbed up and down as Casey nodded vigorously. "Okay then, let's get to it." She reached for the book that Casey kept on the nightstand, the official resting place for each storybook she read to him. "When we left off…" she began.

* * *

"So, how was it?" Marcus finally asked as he brought the sports car he'd bought for himself against Marjorie's objections. At his age and success level, he felt he deserved at least one toy.

He'd picked Ian up at the shelter at the appointed time. His friend had gotten in without saying anything. Now several blocks had gone by and still nothing. Marcus didn't know if Ian was lost in the revelry of creation, or in the depths of the black depression that on occasion overwhelmed him.

Because he cared about Ian, Marcus pushed rather than retreated, even though the latter would have been his natural inclination.

After a beat, Ian looked at him. The shrug was casual. "All right, I guess. Hell of a wake-up call, being among the have-nots again." Ian laughed softly to himself. Even the words sounded as if they were meant for him alone and not the man beside him. "Wasn't all that long ago I was there."

"You worked your tail off not to be stuck at that level," Marcus reminded him, thinking back to the lean and hungry days his friend had endured. Unlike him, Ian had not been born to money. "You pulled yourself up by sheer grit alone."

Sheer grit and luck, Ian thought. True luck had come in the form of his first agent, an older woman by the name of Lola Nash who had seen the potential in that first work of his and worked hard to help him mine it. They lived together for two years before he left, with her blessings. During that time, he wrote three more books. He had climbed to the pinnacle of the bestseller charts by the time the ink was dry on the second one. Success and adulation had been his playmates ever since, but he never managed to shed the person he'd been.

"Doesn't change the fact that those are my roots." He sighed, closing his eyes as he leaned back against the headrest. "We were damn near close to bankruptcy just before the earthquake."

"You were ten years old when the quake hit." It was a neutral way of wording it. Marcus never said anything about Ian's family being killed. Except for once, that first time, they never talked about the tragic accident that had rendered him an orphan. Ian avoided any reference to death altogether—except when he was writing. "How the hell would you know something like that?" Marcus wanted to know. "Most kids don't know anything about their family's finances at that age."

"Ed told me," Ian replied, his tone flat.

He never referred to either of his grandparents by anything other than their first names. As if the only ties between him and them were on paper, recorded in long-forgotten government logs. There were no emotional bonds between him and his mother's parents. Oh, when she'd died, he had turned up at Louise's funeral. Mostly out of respect because the woman had done her best to forgive him for whose son he'd been. But standing there at her grave, he'd felt nothing. No sense of loss, no sadness. He was just an observer and Louise's death was just another rite of passage, nothing more.

It had been a different matter when Lola suddenly passed on. He'd experienced real grief then. But even so, he'd anticipated losing her. Because being abandoned in one fashion or another was a recurring pattern in his life.

Marcus frowned. "Never liked that old man," he confided.

"Ed did his best," Ian said, emotionless.

"I guess." Marcus agreed in order to avoid an argument. In his opinion, though, Ed Humboldt could have done more, much more for his only living blood relation. However, Ian didn't sound as if he was in the mood to rehash past transgressions and sins.

Besides, they'd reached their destination. Marcus pulled up into the driveway and threw the car into park, though he kept the engine idling. "We're here," he announced.

Ian opened his eyes and waited for that feeling of homecoming to overtake him. Tonight, it took its time. He didn't bother analyzing why. "So we are," he murmured under his breath.

Marcus studied him for a moment. "Want me to come in with you?"

Ian smiled. "Don't worry, old friend, I'm not going to do anything stupid." Because he knew that Marcus was going to say something about the original incident that had gotten him into having to do community service, he added, "It's not on my agenda tonight." Stretching, he winced slightly. A twinge had scampered up his back. "I just want a hot shower. That little go-getter at the shelter had me exercising muscles I'd forgotten I had."

"Little go-getter?" Marcus echoed. There was no missing the sudden note of interest in his voice.

"Down, boy," Ian instructed. "It's not what you think. If I had to make a judgment, I'd say that the lady hates my guts."

Marcus found that hard to believe. But there were some who were completely turned off by the worlds within the pages of Ian's books. "Not a fan, huh?"

He shook his head. It went beyond that. "I don't think she knows who I am."

"I take it she's been living under a rock."

Ian could always count on Marcus's loyalty. It was heartwarming even at the worst of times. "Hey, there are people in this world who don't read science fiction," he pointed out. "And if they don't, then my name doesn't mean anything to them. Either name," he added. His own or the one he wrote under. Opening the passenger door, Ian got out of the car and then leaned over to look at Marcus. "It's kind of nice being anonymous again."

"Careful what you wish for." Marcus paused a second, wondering whether he should ask, then decided he had nothing to lose. "Speaking of which, how's the writer's block coming along?"

Ian straightened and blew out a breath. The chill in the air momentarily gave it form, but then it dissipated again.

"Great, just great." He looked at Marcus again. "About the size of the Wall of China right now."

"Oh." It was clear by his expression that Marcus had been hoping to hear the exact opposite. "Well, it'll go away, it always does." He changed the subject. "What time do you want me to swing by tomorrow? I've got to be in court by ten, so—"

But Ian shook his head, interrupting. "Sleep in, Marcus," he told his friend. "I've hired a driver. He starts tomorrow."

It was reported that Ian was the guest every hostess wanted at her party, the life and breath of every gathering. But that was the public Ian. The private one, the real Ian Malone, liked to keep to himself. He had no assistants, no entourage. All came under the heading of invasion. So did a driver.

Marcus knew that Ian had hired the driver so as not to be a burden to anyone. "There's no need for that. I can take you wherever you need to go. And if I'm busy, Marjorie can—"

There was nothing but affection in Ian's voice as he turned down the offer. "I know what you're doing,

Marcus, but I don't need a babysitter. What happened last month was just a temporary break with reality, not something I intend to do on any kind of a regular basis." He laughed, remembering. "The holding cell was bad enough, there's no way I'd do anything that could wind up making me a guest of the county indefinitely. Really," he added when he saw the skeptical expression on his friend's face. "Cross my heart and hope to die." He made an *X* over his chest and then held up his right hand, as if taking the oath.

Marcus still looked unconvinced. "Yeah, it's the last part that worries me."

"Well, don't let it," Ian instructed.

He took in a lungful of crisp, fresh air. The days looked like summer, but the nights told the truth. Autumn was already here and leaning toward winter. The holidays would be here before he knew it. Another Thanksgiving and Christmas to endure. He could feel the specter of pain already.

"If I go out, Marcus, it'll be in style, at the height of my career. Not in the middle of a dry spell like this." He closed the passenger door firmly. "Go home to Marjorie, Marcus." A smile flashed across his lips. "And tell her she married a great guy."

Marcus took the vehicle out of Park and threw it into reverse. "She already knows that."

"Remind her anyway."

With that, Ian backed away. He watched a

moment as the other man straightened the wheel and finally pulled out of the driveway.

"'Night, Marcus," he murmured, turning toward the house that *Architectural Digest* referred to as a mini-mansion when they featured it on their cover last year.

Ian disarmed the security code and let himself in. Rearming it again, he debated leaving all the lights off. The way they were inside of him. But then he decided that keeping them off was just inviting more dark thoughts. He began by turning on the hall light. And then the one in the living room. He made his way to the one in the mini-chandelier in the dining room. And then the group of ceiling lights that graced his kitchen. The ones in the family room were next.

The only light he left off on the first floor was the one in his office, located at the back of the house just off the kitchen.

When he approached the room, he thought about throwing the switch. But he couldn't make himself do it. If he turned on the light, he'd see his computer. And the monitor that had been empty all these weeks. Waiting for something to slip across its screen.

Waiting in vain.

He headed for the stairs. There was plenty of time tomorrow for recriminations. Right now, he had a progressively achier body to tend to.

Chapter Five

"I thought maybe I scared you away."

Startled, Lisa turned from the supply closet to find Ian standing almost directly behind her, a pleased, sensual curve to his mouth. And an amused glint in his eyes.

With her back against the shelves, she had nowhere to go, no room to retreat. For a moment the man and his rangy body took up the space around her.

Lisa hadn't been to the shelter for several days, but that was neither her fault nor her choice. Life kept filling up her days and nights with incidentals, hardly leaving enough time for her to draw two breaths together, much less anything else.

To the eternal joy of her son and the students in her third-grade class, Halloween was swiftly approaching and preparations second only to those involved in staging the royal wedding of Queen Victoria to her Prince Albert were underway. That meant making endless lists, getting supplies, decorating the house *and* the classroom. And, in spare moments, sew the costumes. Casey's, hers and the two boys in her class who were being raised by male single parents, both of whom thought that needles were only something that doctors used to inject antibiotics.

But Halloween was also a holiday the children at the shelter were secretly looking forward to and she didn't want them being disappointed or shortchanged. They had been disappointed by so much already, giving them a party was the least she could do.

So here she was, running almost on empty, sleeping even less than usual, hoping to get something going with a few of the other volunteers in preparation for the big day.

Narrowing her eyes, she gave him a look that clearly told Ian to get out of her way. "Why would you think you could scare me?"

After a beat, thinking that this woman was a hell of a firebrand, Ian obligingly stepped back. But not before he took the stack of papers from her. "You haven't been here in a few days."

Surrendering the pile she intended to use to make

decorative posters, Lisa led the way back to the common room. "And you've been here every day?"

He fell back for a moment, enjoying the view from the rear. Then he lengthened his stride again so that he could walk beside her.

"Those are the terms of the agreement Marcus hammered out for me," he told her.

Marcus. His lawyer, she recalled. Lisa nodded toward the table, indicating he should deposit the stack there. "Must put a crimp in your life, coming here every day."

The stack he placed on the table consisted of colored construction paper as well as white sheets intended for a printer. Absently, he wondered what she was up to. A project to entertain the kids? "Not really. I'm self-employed."

She crossed her arms before her, evaluating his words. Reading between the lines. As a teacher, she was privy to some interesting, creative stories at times and had learned how to separate the truth from fiction. "Is that another way of saying you're out of work?"

"No, that's another way of saying I'm self-employed," he told her, his tone mild. And then, because they had started to haunt him, he thought of the recurring blank screens on his computer. He dreaded even sitting down at his desk because he anticipated the outcome: nothing. "Although, technically, I guess you could say that I'm out of work until I produce something."

Her eyes swept over him. He was dressed casually, but there was the air of money about him. Somebody's rich son, never having had to work a day in his life? She told herself it didn't matter who he was, as long as he did what was required of him—and was made to realize that he couldn't wiggle out of it.

But for the sake of conversation, she asked, "And what is it that you produce?"

The question wasn't coy, he realized. The petite brunette really didn't know who he was. For a moment, he thought of telling her, recalling all the years he'd longed to be able to tell people he was a writer in something other than theory. That he wrote things other people—lots of other people—read. But once that actually happened, once he was published and his books received enthusiastic recognition if not always favorable reviews, the feeling of validation that he had been expecting, that he'd been anticipating with almost a burning need, didn't come.

After all that, he was still who he'd been, the only survivor of a terrible tragedy that had taken the rest of his family and left only him. Left him to find his way in a cold, loveless world and to try to figure out why he hadn't been taken and they had.

With the success of his first book, he realized reaching goals wasn't the answer for him. That, more than likely, there *were* no answers for him. Only existence.

Her not knowing who he was brought him back to the years he'd spent drenched in anonymity. Back then, he'd chafed against it. Now, in hindsight, his view had changed. Maybe anonymity wasn't such a bad thing after all, he mused.

"Nothing right now," he admitted. And then his mouth curved. "Which means I have a lot of time to atone for my transgression."

She was sure that he was accustomed to his smile melting the women around him. It was certainly powerful enough and sexy enough to accomplish that. But she felt she could see through him. He was someone who used others—and his considerable good looks—to get whatever it was he wanted.

Well, it didn't work like that around here. And certainly not around her.

Her temper flared. "You think this is a joke, don't you?"

His tone was nothing but mild. It just goaded her more. "I never said that."

"Not in so many words," she retorted, "but it's in your attitude."

To her surprise—and annoyance—he laughed. "Kitty, you've known me maybe a handful of minutes all told." And then his smile—and the dimple with it—faded. "You have no idea what my attitude is."

She stood her ground. Life had not been easy for her and she had fought battles to overcome soul-draining events to get to where she was. This hotshot was not going to get the upper hand and just coast.

"Think again, Malone. You're not that deep."

Rather than annoy him, Ian found himself amused by her. "Ouch. Are you this rough on everyone who volunteers here?" He took a step closer to her, cutting into her space again. "Or am I special?"

She began to back away, then realized what she was doing and how it had to look to him. As if she were afraid. Lisa planted her feet firmly on the floor. "Number one, you didn't volunteer, you were sent here by a judge. Number two, you're not special. What you are," she concluded, "is dangerous."

To her growing annoyance, she saw the smile return. Anger made her warm. "I take it you don't mean that in a sensual way."

She was in no mood for this. She'd come to work, not to verbally spar with the likes of Malone. But now that this was out on the table, she had to see it through. And be done with it.

"I mean that in a life and death way. As in dangerous to others." Out of the corner of her eye, she saw a few people walk in from the opposite end of the room. She lowered her voice, turning her back toward them. There was no need to make this public, even though her feelings on the subject were a matter of record. "You want to kill yourself, that's one thing, but being behind the wheel with anything but one hundred percent of your faculties and your complete focus when it means you can kill someone else is downright criminal."

He watched her for a long moment. "This is personal, isn't it?"

Her eyes darkened to almost an emerald green. "You don't know me well enough to ask that."

He laughed shortly. "Lady, you just attacked me with a tongue that's sharp enough to split rails at thirty paces, I think I deserve to know why."

His world needed broadening. His sense of entitlement was getting under her skin. "You don't *deserve* anything," she informed him tersely. "Cavalier people like you never do." The words came out before she could stop them. "Someone just as thoughtless as you killed my son's father."

"Your husband?"

The question carved into her heart. She never had the opportunity to call Matt her husband. "He would have been, had he lived another three days." Matt died on a Thursday. They were going to be married that Saturday. "Someone celebrating a whole lot more than he should have plowed his Camaro right into Matt's twelve-year-old sedan. The driver didn't even remember hitting him."

She dug her nails into her palms, trying hard not to let the emotion churning inside spill out.

"Matt died at the scene. He didn't even live long enough for me to tell him that we were going to have a baby." It was hard keeping her voice low and under control. "Someone like you robbed my son of his father and me of my life, so excuse me if I don't have any sympathy for you."

He nodded slowly. Okay, so she had a reason to vivisect him with her tongue. But he had reasons, too, reasons for doing what he did, stupid though it might seem in hindsight.

"Want to hear my side of it?"

Lisa tossed her head. "You don't get a side," she retorted, walking away from him.

He didn't reach for her, didn't try to catch up to her. Instead, Ian remained where he was, leaning against the long table.

"You're lucky, you know."

The words hung in the air without adornment.

How dare he?

Lisa spun around on her heel. "Lucky?" she echoed incredulously, so angry she could spit nails. "I'm *lucky?*" Furious, she made her way back to him. "How the hell do you figure that?"

"At least you have a person to blame, a cause to espouse." He shrugged. From where she stood, the movement looked so calculated as to appear careless. "If I want to attain that same feeling, I've got no one but God to blame. God and nature."

"What are you talking about?"

This was where he walked away. Because this was where he ordinarily shut down. But she had exposed her wounded soul to him and that had triggered something within him, something that had demanded a release for so long.

Without planning to, Ian heard himself saying, "I'm talking about a ten-year-old boy trapped in a car crushed by a freeway underpass pillar, lying for hours beside the body of his dead sister and her dead friend, with his parents dead in the front seat."

Stunned, Lisa stared at him in silence, trying to assimilate the words he was sending her way. "Earthquake?" she finally asked.

He barely nodded his head. To this day, just hearing the word made everything inside of him tighten like a fist braced to swing and make the most of the contact. "Palm Springs."

She remembered the Palm Springs quake. Remembered waking up in her bed to feel it walking across the room, from one wall to another. She'd screamed for her mother. It was over in a matter of seconds—except for the people in Palm Springs, many of whom had found themselves homeless in an instant.

"How did you get out?" she asked quietly.

"What makes you think it was me?" he asked. She couldn't read his expression. "Maybe I'm just yanking your chain, telling you a story."

He could be, but something told her he wasn't. Lisa shook her head. "No, not even you could be that insensitive and obnoxious." She smiled when she said it.

"Does this mean we've got some kind of truce going?"

Lisa lifted a shoulder, then let it drop. "Some kind," she echoed.

"For the record," he said out of the blue, "I took the back roads that night I was arrested. I wasn't out to hurt anyone but me."

To his surprise, he saw concern in her eyes. "Why would you want to hurt yourself?"

Ian shoved his hands into his pockets. "Because I can't answer why."

"Why what?"

He would have been more comfortable avoiding her eyes, but instead he looked directly into them. "Why them and not me."

"Maybe the answer isn't anything you can grab onto now. Maybe it's something that'll be clear to you eventually. Later." They were on her home ground now—optimism. "Maybe you were meant to stay alive because you're going to do something when you're older, save someone, solve the mystery of life, have a son or daughter who changes the course of things in time. You just don't know. None of us do." That was how she kept going herself, after Matt died. Some good had to come of all this pain eventually. "None of us get to look in the back of the book for the answers, we've just got to operate on faith." She saw the grin spread, slowly, sensually along his lips, and found that even though she struggled hard, she was not immune to it. "What?" she finally asked.

"Is this the part where you pass around the collection plate?"

Just when she was beginning to see him in a more favorable light, she thought. Was he deliberately trying to irritate her and put her off? "I wasn't aware that I was preaching."

"You're not," he allowed casually, "but what you just said certainly sounds like something I'd expect to hear in one of those storefront churches that pop up in every city."

Lisa set her mouth hard. "Nothing wrong with faith."

"Didn't say there was."

"You didn't have to," she retorted. "Your mocking tone did."

He shook his head, a tolerant amusement curving his mouth. "Kitty, you keep accusing me of things and seem to fancy yourself on some inner track to my thoughts. I'm sorry to disappoint you, but even I don't know what's going on in there half the time. And if I don't, I'm willing to bet that you sure as hell don't." He put his hand out to her. When she made no effort to shake it, he laughed, his amusement growing. "I'm offering you a truce, Kitty, not waiting to arm wrestle."

"A truce," Lisa repeated, suspicion glimmering in her eyes.

"Yes, you know," he coaxed, "like a cease-fire. It could be a whole lot more pleasant than constantly looking over your shoulder, worrying about sniper fire."

Meaning her, she thought, because his was not a tongue that was razor-sharp. His was more like one dipped in honey, given to charming a person's defenses away rather than slicing through them.

Lisa lifted her chin, defiance in every breath she took. "I'm not afraid."

The grin remained. It was the kind that could draw the bolts out of a battle cruiser and sink her. "I wasn't thinking about you."

Which left him. She tried to ignore the grin, but couldn't. It was, among other things, damn infectious. And she had to admit he was right. A pleasant situation was much easier to work in than an explosive one. If he was telling her the truth, she could see where Malone's demons might get to him.

Lisa pictured herself in his place. It had to have been horrible, pinned down, unable to do anything, with everyone he cared about lying within inches of him. Dead. She thought of Casey in that situation. Her emotions threatened to overwhelm her. She immediately shut them down.

Taking a deep breath, she placed her hand in his. "Okay. Truce."

Malone held her hand a beat longer than he felt he should. A beat longer for him and way too long for her. Because even as their hands touched, as flesh pressed against flesh, she felt some kind of a pull, some sort of electricity, strong and hard, flashing between them.

Lisa pulled her hand away as if she'd just been burned. Damn, he looked amused again, she thought.

"Static?" Ian raised one eyebrow higher than the other in mild curiosity.

Lisa tried to seem nonchalant. "What?"

"Static," Ian repeated. When she still said nothing, he elaborated. "You pulled your hand back as if you'd just gotten a jolt of static electricity."

She grabbed at the excuse. "Right. That's what it was. Static electricity." It was plausible. What else could it be? she reasoned. She cleared her throat, eager to move on. "All right, now that that's out of the way, how are you at decorating?"

"Depends on what," he replied. "Cakes? Windows? Women?"

Lisa wasn't even going to ask what he meant by that last part. Instead, she put her hands on her hips as she turned from him and scanned the large, drab room. Known as the common room, it doubled for so many other things. Classes were given here. Classes to teach mothers how to care for their children, to teach others the basics of life that would see them to securing a job, to putting food on a table and eventually, to getting a table of their own.

On rare occasions, parties took place in this room.

Parties even when there was precious little to cele-
brate. That was what she was thinking of right now.
A party. Something to entertain the children who
would not be allowed to go trick or treating on their
own. This neighborhood was not the kind that concerned itself with the innocence of childhood.

"Walls," she finally said. "Decorating walls with
drawings of cats and pumpkins."

"Halloween?" It didn't exactly take a stretch to
figure out where she was going with this.

She nodded, turning around to face him again.
"That's the holiday."

Of the three holidays at the end of the year, Halloween was the most harmless one in Ian's estima-
tion. Come the big night, he would leave bowls of
candy at the beginning of his winding driveway. That
way, he didn't have to deal with children making
their way to his door. Didn't have to deal with
memories of better times, when Brenda would help
him dress up and then take him around the neighborhood where they lived.

Thanksgiving, and especially Christmas, cut
huge pieces out of his heart, but Halloween just
made him nostalgic.

Ian shook his head. His artistry ended with what
he could do with a keyboard and even that was in
doubt of late. "I think that whatever you're planning
would be more of a success if you put me in charge
of the refreshments."

She was doing her best not to come on like a control freak. "For the record, I wasn't going to *put* you in charge of anything, I was just going to ask what you could do to contribute—"

"That's simple, then," he cut in. "I'll bring the treats."

She nodded. "All right, I'll get a tally of how many kids—"

"I know how many kids are here," he told her, then felt a sliver of satisfaction at her surprised reaction. "I like being on top of things," he said, answering the unspoken question.

She had absolutely no doubt that he did, Lisa thought, then quickly shut down her mind before it could take the thought to its logical conclusion.

Chapter Six

It had been a long time since he'd had a costume on, a long time since he'd allowed himself to give Halloween anything more than a passing thought. This so-called holiday was the beginning of the season he liked the least.

But here he was, Ian thought, looking like some misplaced cowboy in boots and jeans, wearing the fringed jacket and Stetson he'd picked up on his last visit to Houston, sitting in the backseat of the sedan he was forbidden by law to drive for another three months. On the seat next to him there were several shopping bags overflowing with candy.

His driver, Dan McGee, glanced into the rearview

mirror. The man was affable and seemed to be able
to read his passengers' minds. He spoke or kept
silent according to what he discerned.

Ian met Dan's eyes. He couldn't tell if it was
amusement or just plain curiosity he saw reflected
in the man's brown eyes.

"It's for the kids at the shelter," he said need-
lessly, since that was where he'd instructed Dan to
drive him. "You want some for your own kids?" he
asked, remembering that Dan had mentioned he
had two sons, both under the age of eleven. Ian
glanced at the bounty he'd picked up earlier today,
using shopping as an excuse not to write. Procras-
tination had become an art form and making up
excuses was the only creating he did of late.
"There's plenty here, you can have what's left
over." He heard Dan laugh as the latter took a
corner. "I say something funny?"

Easing over into the middle lane, Dan glanced
over his shoulder for half a beat. "Don't know many
kids, do you, Mr. Malone?"

He'd told Dan to call him Ian several times since
Dan had started driving him, but somehow they had
always wound up back at "Mister."

"No," Ian admitted. Before the shelter, his inter-
action with children had been extremely limited.
Apparently it showed. "Why?"

"There *are* no leftovers when it comes to candy
and kids, especially chocolate," the driver noted,

nodding at the bags he'd helped deposit into the rear of the vehicle after picking Ian up at the mall.

"Then I'd better let you take what you want before I bring them into the shelter."

There was genuine warmth in Dan's voice. "That's really nice of you, Mr. Malone."

Gratitude always embarrassed him. Since he couldn't ignore it, he shrugged it off. "No big deal," Ian murmured. "It's only candy."

But it wasn't "only" candy. It was Botticelli, a superrich, super-exclusive chocolate that sold for five cents less than thirty dollars a pound.

Ian figured it would go over well with the kids. If their teeth were going to rot, it might as well be done with the best.

Lisa zeroed in on the name and logo embossed on the sides of the shopping bags the moment Ian and his driver walked into the common room. Immersed in last-minute decorations, trying to keep an eye on her son while she made sure that everything was ready for the party, her mouth dropped open when she saw the "treats" that Ian had brought to the party.

Couldn't the man take simple instruction?

The last of the crepe paper in her hand, Lisa crossed the floor to Ian, a colorful stream marking her path behind her.

"Botticelli's?" she cried, stunned. She looked at him as if he had lost his mind.

Now what? Ian's impatience swirled through him. He'd deliberately given up his afternoon to go to the mall and stand for almost an hour inside the trendy shop, waiting to pay for his purchases. Obviously he still wasn't able to read this woman.

"Yes, Botticelli's. What's wrong?" he asked, turning toward the sound of her voice.

It was the first time he saw her costume. The first time, he later realized, that he actually *saw* her. For a split second, he lost his train of thought and his breath. The voice was definitely Lisa Kittridge's, but as for the rest of her, well, it took him several moments to get his bearings, several seconds to put the voice and the figure together.

And what a figure.

The woman standing before him was wearing a small black mask that seemed somehow incredibly sexy. Instead of being smooth and pulled back, her long, dark hair was a torrent of waves. A multicolored skirt enticingly hugged her hips then fanned out in a profusion of rainbows while a dozen or so bracelets on each bare arm softly created music with every move she made. The small, tightly laced black velvet vest stood out against her white peasant blouse.

Ian couldn't help wondering if she knew that it dipped a little with each breath she took. And that each time it did, he found his pulse racing, echoing the rhythm of her breath.

"Nothing," she said with a resigned, weary sigh, "if you're planning on dating these kids."

She supposed she couldn't blame him. The man obviously had no experience with this sort of thing. And his long-term memory hadn't held up well. But then, most adults didn't remember what it had been like to be a kid. She sighed again, shaking her head as she looked through the first shopping bag. The chocolate probably cost more than she saw in a week as a teacher.

She raised her eyes to his. "This is much too expensive to be used for Halloween candy."

Well, expensive or not, it was all he had to offer at the moment. Ian had a feeling it was too late to make a run to the local grocery store, even if he were so inclined.

"The people at Botticelli's didn't seem to think so," he told her. Turning toward his driver, he said, "Just put the rest of the bags down there, Dan." He deposited his own beside the table on the floor. Dan followed suit, then retreated.

"I'll be waiting in the car, sir," the driver informed him.

Lisa didn't wait for Ian to contradict him. "No," she protested, surprising both men. "Stay. It's cold outside."

Dan's brown eyes shifted over toward the man signing his weekly checks. Ian spread his hands in careless gesture. He hadn't meant to make it sound as if he were banishing Dan to the frozen tundra.

"Sure, stay." Ian glanced over to the wild gypsy beside him. Why hadn't he ever noticed how petite she was? Or how vivid? "I didn't think you'd let just anyone hang out here."

The smile that curved her generous mouth told him that she viewed him as just this side of mentally challenged.

"It's a shelter, Malone. Anyone can stay here, especially to get out of the cold." Getting back to business, Lisa looked down at the five overflowing bags on the floor and shook her head, her bracelets clanging as she fisted her hands at her waist. "You could have bought three times as much for what you spent on this. Maybe four."

His expression gave nothing away. "And then they'd get sick to their stomachs and you'd blame me for that. Can't win, can I?"

Mentally, she recoiled, her conscience stinging her. Was that how she came across to him? A harpy? "I'm sorry, I didn't mean to sound as if I wasn't grateful." Crouching, she sifted through the small neatly wrapped figures. Each one looked like a small work of art. This was going to be wasted on the under-fifteen set. "It's just that you could have saved yourself some money."

"It's mine to spend," he pointed out. As Lisa began to rise, he took her elbow, helping her up. Her eyes met his and he dropped his hand to his side. Maybe he was getting a wee bit too familiar for her taste, he decided. "And this way," he plucked a black vampire wrapped in clear cellophane from the top of the bag and held it up for her inspection, "they'll have something to remember."

There was no arguing with that, she supposed. "That they will." Beckoning over one of the volunteers she'd recruited for party duty, she deadpanned, "Guard those with your life."

Lisa directed one quick glance over toward her son to make sure he was still playing with several of the boys she'd introduced him to—he was—before she turned back to her task. The party started in less than half an hour and there was still punch to make.

"By the way," she said as she walked back to the table and the punch bowl she'd retrieved earlier from the rafters over her two-car garage, "Thanks for dressing up."

"I was going to say the same thing to you."

The comment was said under his breath and not really intended for anyone—especially her—to hear. When she turned around to look at him, he realized his voice carried more than he thought it did.

For a second, he held his breath, wondering if he was in for a lecture about sexism or something equally damning. But the amused expression on her face reassured him.

"Well, don't just stand there looking rugged," she said after a beat. "I need a hand in the kitchen."

He would have preferred giving her a hand in the

bedroom. The thought came literally out of nowhere. This time, mercifully, he kept his response from coming to his lips.

"Which one, right or left?" he quipped.

She never missed a beat. "Either one will do."

The next moment, he realized that he wasn't the only one dancing to her attendance. Dan was right behind him as he followed her to the kitchen.

The lady was good, Ian thought. In exchange for a little warmth and a well-placed smile, she'd managed to get herself some extra volunteer labor.

Without realizing it, he began thinking of her in terms of a character he could use in one of his stories. His next one. Provided that there was ever going to *be* a next one.

Dan, it turned out, was a wonderful asset to the party. Muriel and the tall, burly driver conducted games for the children while parents sat by and watched. At least for a little while, families could feel as if they were average people and that everything was as it should be.

After checking for the third, possibly the fourth time to make sure that the candy bowls were amply refilled, Lisa sank down in a chair beside Ian. The latter, she noted, had just replenished the punch bowl as she'd asked.

He was coming along, she thought grudgingly.

The wall of intermingling voices and laughter

warmed her, making her feel as if she'd done something good. The children needed this, she firmly believed that with all her heart. They needed this, and so did their parents.

She needed this as well, she realized, needed to feel as if she had accomplished something. That for a small island of time she had managed to banish everyone's worries and allowed them to enjoy themselves. The world would be with them all too soon.

Glancing around the room, she searched for Casey. As always, there was that slight mental pause, that slight pricking of nerves until she finally spied him. Typical mother thing, she told herself. The couple of times Casey had darted away from her in a department store, to play his own version of hide-and-seek, she had aged ten years. Both times.

She saw him and let out her breath as inconspicuously as possible. Casey was playing with three other children, taking the lead as he had a tendency to do. This time, he'd probably blame it on his costume. He'd come as Wolverine, which clearly made him a leader, she thought with a smile she didn't bother to conceal.

All the children wore some sort of costume, she made sure of that. What she hadn't gotten by way of donations, she'd gotten by recruitment, talking several of her friends into giving up a few hours in order to fashion a costume for a child. It was intended to keep them from feeling different.

No child left behind, she thought with a smile. *At least not for tonight.*

Ian watched her face in fascination as expression after expression came and went. He couldn't help wondering if she was aware that all her thoughts registered across her face.

Because it was so noisy, he leaned forward and then said against her ear, "You organize a great party."

Lisa's mouth curved even deeper. "The kids are the ones who make it a great party," she countered.

There was no denying, though, that she was well pleased with what she was witnessing. Children having fun, making the most of the moment. She helped with that, she thought, embracing the silent words. And then, because it was a cause that was near and dear to her heart, she couldn't help adding, "This is so much better than going trick-or-treating door to door."

He was surprised to hear her say that. "Knocking an American institution?" he asked mildly.

Lisa laughed shortly under her breath. "It just never made all that much sense to me," she admitted.

In the short time that he had been interacting with her, he'd learned that her mind had a habit of jumping around. He wanted to make sure he followed this thread of a conversation. "Trick or treating?"

Lisa nodded. "Three hundred and sixty-four days

a year, we tell our kids not to talk to strangers and especially not to take candy from strangers. Then one day a year—at night, no less—we tell them, 'Go,'" she snapped her fingers, "'knock yourselves out. Take candy from strangers.'"

Pointing out that parents usually went with their small children and that the doors knocked on belonged to neighbors would probably seem argumentative to her, so he refrained, asking only, "Is that why you brought your son here?"

She hadn't introduced Casey to him, or even pointed him out to Malone. "How did you…?"

"I heard him call you Mommy. Nice-looking boy from what I can see." Most of her son's face was hidden by his mask and headgear, but the boy definitely had her smile, there was no missing that.

As if to prove it, Lisa smiled warmly. "Thank you. I think so."

She glanced at her watch. The party had gone on a little more than two hours now. She was going to wind it down soon. Some of the younger children, her son included, needed to get to bed.

And there was still clean up to face, she thought, resigning herself to it.

As she began to get up, she saw one of the little girls stuff an entire tiny chocolate haunted house into her mouth. "What made you bring such expensive candy?" she asked, suddenly turning toward Ian.

She'd promised herself not to ask again, but her

curiosity got the better of her. Most men would have just grabbed bags of anything they saw in the seasonal aisle in the supermarket, not gone out of their way to make a trip to the mall for designer chocolate. Especially if their license had been suspended.

Ian shrugged. Two ghosts played tag and one plowed right into him. "Whoa." Catching the child, he turned the specter around and pointed him in the right direction. Accustomed to working in bits and pieces of time, he continued as if they hadn't been interrupted. "I thought as long as they were going to get cavities, it might as well be because they'd eaten the best."

She laughed and shook her head. "I want you to know you're probably going to be responsible for me going bankrupt. Casey told me he wants this candy all the time now."

Ian smiled. "He's got good taste."

The quick jolt she felt caught her completely by surprise. As did the warmth that fed through her veins. She was tired, she reasoned. Tired always equaled vulnerable. Knowing that helped her keep up her defenses. Not looking at his smile helped even more.

"He might have good taste, but he won't be snacking on Botticelli chocolate anytime soon, not while his mother's on a teacher's salary."

Offering to buy the boy some of the exclusive chocolate would probably offend her, he decided. "Then I guess I did something bad?"

A few weeks ago, she might have said yes, or at least been tempted to. But lately, almost against her will, she'd started to look beyond the clever words and snappy attitude to the man who existed beneath them. The man who used all that like a protective shield to keep the world at bay.

"Not intentionally," she allowed. "Your heart was in the right place." Out of the corner of her eye, she saw a couple of the children yawning. And Casey was rubbing his eyes. That was her signal. "Time to wrap this up. You can go home anytime, you know. You've more than put in your time tonight."

He rose to join her. "Thanks, warden, but I think I'll stick around."

She was being bossy again. Her mother kept telling her she had to work on that. "I didn't mean to imply—"

He raised his hand to stop the unnecessary apology. "You need to work on your sense of humor, Kitty." His eyes swept over her appreciatively. There was no point in pretending he didn't notice. "Everything else, though, is letter perfect."

She struggled to keep the smile from her lips. It had been a long time since she'd allow herself to feel like a woman. She supposed the costume was an unconscious part of it. Originally, she'd intended to come as Cinderella's fairy godmother, a lovely woman lost in the folds of old age. Dowdy, not sexy. At the last minute, she'd dug up the costume she'd worn to the party where she had met Matt. She'd told herself—and her mother—that she was wearing the costume purely out of nostalgia.

Her mother had made a little noise when she'd heard the explanation that told Lisa that Susan Kittridge wasn't buying it.

Maybe she wasn't, either, Lisa thought now, slanting a glance at Ian. Maybe she'd worn this costume just to get that kind of a reaction from him.

So now what?

Now she'd gotten it. Time to call it a night and go back to being Lisa Kittridge, supermom. "Okay, you had your chance to escape. If you're going to stay, I'm not going to talk you out of it." She glanced around the room. Every surface seemed to be littered with cups, empty and not, and plates, ditto. "I could use the help."

"No good deed goes unpunished, right?" he asked, amused, as he following her to the gaily decorated main table.

Lisa cast him a glance over her shoulder and tried not to dwell on how rugged he looked. The man was probably a cream puff inside, she told herself. "Something like that."

Clean up, even with a number of the other volunteers and parents pitching in, took more than an hour. By the time everything was back in its place and the decorations had been taken down and stored for another year, Casey was curled up on a chair, sound asleep.

"Looks like Wolverine has decided to let some other superhero do the fighting for him tonight," Ian commented, standing behind Lisa.

"Mutant," Lisa corrected him, slipping Casey's jacket on over his costume. It took a bit of doing. "Wolverine is a mutant."

"My mistake." Ian waited for her to get Casey's other sleeve on. When she began to pick the boy up, he stepped in. "Here, let me."

She had a thing about doing everything herself, about not asking for or accepting help. "He's my son."

Ian heard the defensive note in her voice and found himself wondering, not for the first time, about the woman, her life and what had brought her to this almost compulsion to do good deeds.

He surprised her by not backing off the moment she protested.

"I know that, Kitty. I wasn't about to run off with him," he told her. "I just thought he might be a little heavy after the day you've put in."

"Sorry, didn't mean to be testy. I guess I am tired." She forced a smile to her lips. The man was only trying to help. He wasn't the worthless blotch on society she'd initially taken him for. He was very nice. "It's just that I still have book reports to grade when I get home."

He picked up Casey, who continued to sleep. He had the impression that Lisa's son could be used as a basketball and would still continue to sleep. He walked with Lisa toward the exit. Dan fell into place right behind them.

"The fun just never stops for you, does it?" Ian asked.

Lisa laughed. "No, I guess not."

She pushed one of the double doors and they walked outside. A wave of cold air rushed up to greet them. Before raising her own collar, Lisa paused to tug Casey's up. She thought how getting his jacket over his costume had been no easy feat, especially since Casey had been a lead weight.

The boy would sleep through an earthquake, she mused, then was immediately grateful she hadn't made the comment out loud, remembering what Malone had told her.

"That's my car over there," she pointed toward a ten-year-old Toyota whose luster had begun to fade. The next moment, she hurried ahead of Ian to unlock the vehicle.

"If you're too tired," he called after her, "Dan could drive you home."

She glanced over toward the driver and Ian's own car. "What about you?"

Ian stepped back as she opened the rear passenger seat. He eased Casey down onto the seat and then stepped back as Lisa fastened the seatbelts. "I'd follow in my car," he told her.

Finished, she drew her head back out and looked at him sharply. "That's a violation of the terms of your probation."

"It's for a worthy cause." He grinned. "I could always say the gypsy bewitched me and made me do it."

There went that strange tightening sensation, she thought, trying to ignore it. "Nice try. I'll be fine," she assured him, getting in behind the wheel.

Ian nodded. "Well, good night."

Turning away, he headed toward his own car. Behind him, he heard Lisa start hers. And start it. And start it.

The engine wasn't catching.

He retraced his steps. "Trouble?" he asked, bending down to her opened window.

"Sounds like it," she said with a sigh. Why now? Sitting back, she stopped turning the key and caught her lower lip between her teeth. "I don't suppose you know anything about cars."

Finally, something where he didn't feel like a duck crossing the Arizona desert. He grinned. "Funny you should mention that."

Chapter Seven

"I worked in a garage to put myself through school," Ian said to the gypsy beside him.

Dan, who had sheepishly admitted to her that his knowledge of automobiles began and ended with the dials on the dashboard, was standing beside him, holding a flashlight aloft. The driver angled the flashlight so that the beam illuminated the area beneath the raised hood.

When he'd volunteered to help her, Ian had sent Lisa back into Providence Shelter to borrow a screwdriver and a wrench. She returned within minutes, eager to help. But there was only room for one set of hands within the interior of the engine area.

Besides, when he caught a glimpse of her, the expression on her face indicated that she might as well have been looking into a black hole for all the sense the different engine belts and hoses made to her.

He worked in a garage to put himself through school. He answered Lisa's question, telling her how a man with seemingly soft hands knew his way around distributor caps and fuel injectors.

She turned her head to look at him, a trace of amazement in her eyes. "You *worked* your way through school?"

He imagined that the same tone of incredulity was evident when someone was told that the moon was made of green cheese. He'd thought that he'd already proven that he could work pretty damn hard when the occasion called for it.

"Yes, why? You seemed surprised."

She was. And she'd have to completely scrub that first opinion she'd formed of him. But there was still that careless attitude toward money, she thought.

"It's just that someone who hands out thirty-dollar-a-pound candy doesn't strike me as someone who had to work his way through school."

He laughed. Was that it? "Ever think that might be the reason why someone would be handing out expensive candy? Because he knows firsthand what it's like to do without?"

The answer caught her up short. "No," she admitted after a beat. She inclined her head, giving him the point. "I guess I'd better readjust my thinking." *Maybe even about you,* she added silently.

"I guess so," Ian agreed, making no effort to hide the amusement in his voice. Putting the wrench and the flat-head screwdriver down on the side of the vehicle, he stepped back. "Okay, try it now," he instructed.

Lisa glanced into the backseat as she got in behind the steering wheel. Casey slept as soundly as if he was in his own bed. Thank God for small favors, she thought.

And big ones. This time, when she turned the key, the engine hesitated, then coughed to life. Within seconds, it purred. She sat there for a second, just enjoying the fact that the car was running again.

Lisa left the key in the ignition as she slid out from behind the steering wheel.

"It's alive," she declared with all the verve of Dr. Frankenstein announcing the success of his much-slaved-over experiment.

Ian wiped the grease smudges off his fingers with the bandana he'd pulled out of his back pocket. He was getting a kick out of her reaction. It beat having her scowling at him.

"The connection to the battery terminals was loose," he informed her. "Not to mention that there was all sorts of gunk on them." He'd carefully scraped off as much as he could from the two cylin-

drical rods. "When was the last time you had the terminals cleaned?"

"Cleaned?" she echoed. It had never occurred to
her that what was beneath the hood of an automo-
bile could be cleaned.

Ian laughed and shook his head. "Well, I guess
that answers that. Tell your mechanic he needs to do
a better job servicing your car."

That would be fine, if she had one of those, she
thought. Whenever something was wrong, she'd
have the car towed to the local gas station. Mechan-
ics there came and went, usually because they didn't
know what they were doing.

"I don't have a mechanic," she admitted.

Ian glanced down at the streaked bandana, not
overly eager to slip it back anywhere on his person. For
the time being, he balled it up in his hand. "You do
now."

Her eyes widened as she looked at him. "You?"
Was he serious?

"Why not? I could give it a once-over, tell you
what it needs. You can have someone else do the
work if you like." He had a feeling that she'd
probably prefer that, actually.

She didn't want to insult him, though, especially
since he'd come to her rescue like an old-fashioned
cowboy. "No, I trust you. It's just that, well, don't
you have better things to do with your time?"

He would have, he thought ruefully. If he could

just get past this damn writer's block that seemed to be growing each day, like some giant marshmallow on steroids. It was all but smothering him now.

He shrugged away her concern. "Not in the near future."

His answer piqued her curiosity. What *was* it that this man did for a living? He'd already told her that he was self-employed, but self-employed doing what? She'd never managed to pin him down about that. She had just assumed that he dabbled in order to keep from thinking of himself as numbering among the idle rich. But then, if he'd had to work his way through school, that meant that somewhere along the line, there had been a shortage of money.

"But soon," he added vaguely, more for his own benefit that for hers. "I'll probably be at it again soon."

The truth was, he'd been saying that to himself for more than the last nine months. The deadlines that had loomed in the future were growing closer and closer, feeding a mounting uneasiness. He wondered if whatever talent he'd been blessed with had mysteriously vanished.

Ian came closer to the driver's side, bending down so that he could speak to her through the window she'd rolled down. The wind shifted and a hint of the cologne she wore found him.

Nice, he thought.

He tapped the roof. "Looks like you're good to go," he told her.

Thanks to you, she thought. She smiled at him, feeling guilty for all the negative thoughts she'd had about him. "Thank you."

He shrugged off the thanks. "We could follow you," he told her. "Just to make sure that the car continues to run."

Automobiles were nothing if not unpredictable. It gave them something in common with the fairer sex, he thought.

She definitely didn't want to put him out any more than she already had. For all she knew, he had somewhere to go after this. A party to attend, a girlfriend waiting for him. So she shook her head, declining his offer. "I'm sure you fixed whatever needed fixing."

He reached into his jacket pocket, took out his wallet and pulled out a piece of paper from it. "Got a pen?" he asked her.

Curious, she reached over to the glove compartment and opened it. There were a couple of pens in the crease where the door met the dashboard. She handed one to him, then watched him write something down.

Finished, he surrendered the pen and pressed the paper into her hand. "Here, just in case."

She looked at the paper. It was too dark to make it out. "What's this?"

"My cell phone number. Call if you find yourself stuck."

She glanced at it one last time before putting it on the seat beside her. "You're scaring me."

A beautiful woman out alone and unprotected in a car with her five-year-old at night could be a very scary situation, he thought. A half a dozen different scenarios suggested themselves to him.

"Good," he told her, straightening, "then my work here is done."

With that, he turned away and he and the silent driver who had patiently been waiting for him to finish, walked to the waiting sedan.

"Home, James," Ian instructed, tongue-in-cheek, once he saw Lisa pull out of the parking lot.

"It's Dan," the burly man corrected him as he opened the rear passenger door.

Ian didn't feel like sitting in the back. It made him feel too isolated. Instead, he opened the front passenger door and got in. "Yes, Dan," he said good-naturedly, "I know that."

When Dan brought him home, the first thing that Ian noticed was that the huge bowls of candy he'd left in his wake were conspicuously empty. He figured they would be.

It was a little after eight o'clock and all the children who had a right to be out trick-or-treating were back in their homes with their parents. At this point, the only ones on the streets were costumed occupants of junior high schools or, in one case, what looked and sounded to be a senior in high school. All of whom, he firmly believed, should have been smart enough to find a different way to secure candy for themselves. While costumes were for children of all ages, actual door-to-door trick-or-treating should be the domain of the very young and easily awed, hence the tiny pieces of candy.

It rankled him when preteens and especially teenagers tried to horn in on this territory.

"Trick or treat, Mister," a rather tall ghost said to him in a voice that was deeper than his as he got out of his vehicle.

He saw Dan step forward. Dan, he'd discovered, fancied himself to be not just his driver but also his unofficial bodyguard. He didn't write anything nearly inflammatory enough to warrant a bodyguard, Ian thought, amused as he now shook his head at the other man.

Ian dug into his pocket and took out a dollar bill. He tossed it into the "ghost's" pillowcase. "Here, buy yourself a disposable razor," he instructed, then walked away from the specter, who promptly hurried off in the opposite direction.

"Will you be wanting to go anywhere else tonight, Mr. Malone?" Dan asked, raising his voice.

Ian paused by the front door and shook his head. "No, that's it for tonight." He smiled at the man, although from this angle, he doubted if the driver could see. "You've gone over and above the call of duty, Dan. Go home to your kids. And don't forget to take the candy," he reminded him.

Dan already had the bag filled with chocolate figures in his hand. "Looking forward to sampling some of this myself," he confessed just before he got into his own vehicle, a beige Chevy Nova that had seen better years. "See you tomorrow." Starting up the car, Dan waved and then took off.

"Right," Ian murmured.

Disarming the security alarm, he let himself in, then reengaged the system. The only light on was the one in the foyer.

He stood there for a moment, taking in the silence. The house felt lonelier than usual after all the noise and activity he'd left behind. He caught himself thinking that all it would take to brighten the premises up would be one woman.

The reflection in the window was sporting a half smile. Ian sobered, banishing the thought—and the image of Lisa—from his mind.

"Don't go getting soft on me now," he admonished the reflection.

The last thing he needed was to entertain thoughts about getting intimate with a woman who had a kid and, for the most part, a chip on her shoulder. Of course, it was a very lovely, enticing shoulder, he recalled, thinking about the way she'd looked in her costume tonight. And her son was a rather cute, well-behaved kid as far as that went.

But that didn't change the fact that he'd made himself a promise a long time ago never to get attached to anyone, never to have any sort of feelings that went deeper than the surface.

No ties, no pain, it was as simple as that.

His friendship with Marcus was as close as he intended on getting to anyone and that had evolved more against his will than by any conscious thought on his part. The relationship had initially come into being because they both went to the same elementary school and Marcus had needed help defending himself against bullies.

As a kid, Marcus was short and overweight with glasses and possibly the most awful haircut ever given a human being. The classic victim, he all but had a target painted on his back. Any kid at school with half a mean streak who wanted to act like a big man in front of his friends almost seemed compelled to pick on Marcus and make his life a living hell.

Ian had been the new kid in school, newly transplanted out of a foster home when his grandparents had been informed of his parents' death. He was aware of Marcus and his dilemma almost from the beginning. After watching the stocky boy being picked on for several days running, he'd decided he'd had enough of standing on the sidelines. Besides, he was dying to hit someone. Anyone. As it turned out, hitting wasn't necessary. The bullies were really cowards and they backed off from what they later loudly made known was a crazy person. So Ian had been awarded a reputation as someone to steer clear of, an unstable kid at best, and Marcus had a champion. He'd pledged his undying loyalty immediately. Two outcasts, they became friends slowly only because that had been Ian's choice.

Marcus had stuck by him ever since, no matter what.

With a sigh, Ian walked through the house, turning on lights in an attempt to chase away the demons that seemed to be hiding in every dark corner. It was time to start making plans, he thought, plans to get away for the holidays.

Every year, right around Thanksgiving, he left town. As if that could somehow help banish the anguish that old memories brought.

Marcus always invited him to spend the holidays with his family, but he had never taken his friend up on the offer. Being with Marcus and his family would only remind him that he had no family of his own and that they had been taken from him.

No, if he was going to mingle, it was going to be with a mindless, vapid crowd that couldn't generate a whole thought among the lot of them. Of course, there was a reason for that. No matter where they went, whether it was to the Caribbean, to Valle, or to the south of France, they always partied to excess and drank even more.

With enough alcohol, Ian thought, you could successfully numb any pain.

Without realizing it, he'd worked his way to the back of the house. After turning on the bevy of overhead lights in the kitchen, he found himself standing in the doorway of his office. Going with impulse, he flipped the light switch up. Then down. Then up again. Light winked in and out of the room.

He remained where he was, not venturing in any further. Directly in front of him, with the window looking out onto the backyard at its back, was his computer. He never turned it off, a habit he acquired early on, when ideas would come to him in the middle of the night and he hadn't wanted to waste time, waiting for the computer to warm up.

Now it just stood dormant, waiting. A screen saver in the form of an aquarium with colorful exotic fish filled the surface of the monitor. There were even sound effects, water swishing back and forth. No doubt it was meant to soothe. But in his case, all it did was agitate him.

The steady rhythm seemed to mock him, all but whispering "Slacker, slacker."

He knew that the longer he kept away from work, the longer he didn't try to write, the harder it was going to be to get started. He'd all but given up trying, going for days without so much as even touching the keyboard.

And with each day that passed, the chasm waiting to swallow him up grew larger and larger until it seemed without end. So he backed away, retreating to a safer area and pretended that everything was all right. That when the time came, he would be able to weave his magic.

But now, as he stood here alone, watching the fish swim as aimlessly around as he did, doubts reached up to snare him. Maybe this was the way it was going to be from now on. Maybe he'd only had those seven books in him and now there was nothing more. He was empty.

Maybe, he reasoned, he was on his way to becoming the late, great Ian Malone, aka B. D. Brendan, a once-promising young writer of science fiction.

Do it. Just start with the first step and do it.

The words made Ian jolt. He swore that he'd just heard them spoken out loud, but that was impossible. He was alone here.

And yet…

And yet it sounded like *her* voice. Lisa. Lisa, ordering him around the way she had done at the shelter, sparing no words, soft-pedaling nothing. Pointing out what needed doing and expecting him to do it. Like his replacing the shingles on the roof that first day he'd come to the shelter.

"Easy for you to say," he murmured into the emptiness. "You don't have a reputation you have to live up to."

That was what came of making such a splash with his first book, he thought ironically. People expected you to get better or, at the very least, to be the same, to produce something new and different, but the same. Not slide backward.

That's what he had done with his last book. *Ghosts Among Us*. It was supposed to have been his best offering, but somewhere along the line, he must have lost his way. The problem was, he couldn't see it, couldn't see where he had gone wrong.

Damn it, he thought, shoving his hands into the back pockets of his jeans, he still liked it, *still* thought it was good. Which, he supposed, made him blind.

And made him doubt. In his ability, in his talent, in everything.

At least he had entertained the reviewers. They had had a field day, delighting in writing things such as: "Sadly, the shining light is no more. By foisting this upon his adoring public, Mr. Brendan has betrayed his readers. *Ghosts Among Us* does not live up to the promise of his earlier works. We've plunked down our hard-earned cash only to purchase a lie."

Plunked down hard-earned cash, his butt. The reviewers didn't pay for copies of his book, the publisher sent copies of the book out to them. All they had to do was read it—if they knew how, he thought bitterly. It was damn easy to sit there and pick a book apart. He'd like to see one of those heartless pea-brains try to write a book. They wouldn't get past the title page, if that.

But the criticism still hit home, still burrowed

itself under his skin no matter how much he tried to pretend that it didn't. What bothered him most was the line about not fulfilling his promise. His father had always taught him that if you made a promise, you had to keep it. You were only as good as your word. It was one of the few bits of father advice that had struck with as much as it had.

His publisher hadn't been happy about the reviews, but they didn't pull the plug on him either. They told him that they had faith in him and drew up another contract for a new book. Signatures were put to paper, deadlines arranged. Deadlines that were now threatening to catch up to him.

And still nothing was coming.

Ian sighed, weary. He was too tired to challenge himself tonight even though it really wasn't that late. Maybe tomorrow would be better. Maybe tomorrow the words would come.

With that, he reached into the room again and flipped the light switch off. Darkness fell across the room once more.

The exotic fish continued to meander in circles.

Chapter Eight

As she pulled in, Lisa caught herself scanning the small parking lot that the shelter shared with the dry cleaners. Her search was only in part for a parking space. She was also looking for Ian, or at least his car.

It wasn't there.

She pulled into a space. The quick stab of disappointment annoyed Lisa.

Dear God, she wasn't going to allow herself to get caught up in that tender trap again. Once was lovely, fantastic even, but the downside, the pain, the grief that came down like a heavy anvil when love abruptly left, was overwhelming. She never intended to revisit that feeling.

After getting out, she locked her door and circled around to the front of the building and the entrance. She had her son, she reminded herself, her family, her career. If there were any small slots left to be filled, her work at the shelter more than took care of that.

She had no room in her life for a man, even one with a killer smile and eyes the color of blue smoke; a guy who knew how to fix cars.

She hadn't taken Malone up on his offer, at least not outright. Privacy was very important to her. She hadn't called him, hadn't released her number or address to him so that he could come by and check out the vehicle. There was no doubt in her mind that the vehicle wouldn't have been the only thing Malone would have been willing to check out and she had to admit that lately, she kept feeling as if she was in some sort of a vulnerable, restless state. She had no idea why, it wasn't tied to anything in particular, not a birthday, not an unofficial anniversary, nothing.

Nothing except for the upcoming holidays, she suddenly realized.

Thanksgiving and especially Christmas always made her a little more misty, a little more prone to feeling lost. As far back as she could remember, she'd always loved the holidays, loved the anticipation, loved preparing for them, even when she was a little girl.

But now, the approach of those special days was

a source of deep sadness for her. She went through the motions, so well at times that she doubted if anyone but her mother suspected what was going on inside of her. The elaborate act she put on was primarily for Casey, because he shouldn't have to suffer and miss out on the joy of the season just because his mother felt bereft around this time of year.

As she crossed to the front of the shelter, Lisa tried to shift her thoughts to something positive, something uplifting. Once upon a time, that hadn't been an effort for her. But she missed Matt a great deal around the holidays, even though she'd told herself and everyone else that she had moved on. She might have, but her heart, well her heart hadn't really made the complete journey yet.

For a second, she thought she saw Malone's vehicle parked out front, but then she realized it was the wrong model. She shook her head. At least knowing Malone had been useful for something. Because although she hadn't had him over to her house to give her car the once over, last Friday she'd found him doing it in the parking lot of his own volition.

It had surprised her because he had the hood of her car opened, something she knew was not possible unless he had gotten into her car—and she always kept it locked.

When she'd called out to him, asking how he had gotten into the vehicle, he'd merely smiled that million-dollar smile of his and told her she would be surprised what a person could learn if they just kept their eyes and ears open.

Which made her wonder about him even more.

Her mind went in directions she'd never visited before. Had his money come from dishonest sources?

Did he deal in stolen cars? Drugs? Some kind of black-market dealings?

Lisa knew that she couldn't come right out and ask him, but it was driving her crazy.

Doesn't matter, she told herself, as she walked into the shelter. The heavy door closed behind her with a resounding thud. *Doesn't matter where his money is coming from, this Malone isn't going to figure into your life for very long. Once he serves his time, he's out of here. You know that.*

So many of the people who had been sent to Providence Shelter never came back once their debt to society was paid off.

Malone's punctual arrival surprised her. That he was here more frequently than necessary, according to Muriel, positively amazed her. She'd have thought Malone would have skipped out on sessions whenever possible, citing a variety of creative excuses and flat-out lies.

Instead, Ian was here every time she came to the shelter herself. And he was doing whatever needed doing. Helping with repairs, preparing meals, collecting donated clothing, everything and anything. A lot of things she would have considered beyond his realm.

Yesterday, she'd overheard Muriel telling him to look over their failing boiler, asking him if he could tinker with it and see if he thought it could be saved.

The boiler had solemnly been pronounced dead at 7:45 that evening.

Not a very promising way to face the coming winter, Lisa thought. Even if this was Southern California, it did get cold in the winter evenings. Besides, hot water was a necessity anytime of the year.

As she crossed from the entrance, through the foyer and to the living space beyond, it suddenly struck her that the shelter looked deserted. She actually heard her heels echoing on the vinyl. Ordinarily, she'd at least hear the sound of voices, maybe coming from the common room, the sleeping area or the kitchen. But there was nothing. Not a sound.

She cocked her head. Still nothing.

Where was everyone?

An uneasiness undulated through her. Was something wrong? She could think of half a dozen things that could have emptied out the shelter. A gas leak. The board of health being called in by a disapproving neighbor.

"Hello?" Lisa called.

It was so empty, the sound of her own voice seemed to echo. Feeling nervous, she crossed the common room, then quickly made her way down the narrow corridor to the kitchen.

Raul, a former chef and once homeless, had come to Providence Shelter two years ago. Through patience and a great deal of nurturing care from Muriel and some of the permanent volunteers, Raul had finally found his way back from the abyss where he had resided for so long. Renewed, revived, he'd still had no place to call his own. Muriel had given him a space within the storage room and it suited him fine. In exchange for the bed, he stayed on to work magic in their kitchen.

Standing a little more than five feet tall, with salt-and-pepper hair and a leathery complexion, the slight man nursed something in a large pot on the stove. He looked so intent, she didn't want to bother him. But so far, he was the only one she'd found on the premises.

When he didn't turn around by the time she reached him, Lisa tapped him on the shoulder. "Raul, where is everyone?"

Raul swung around, the ladle in his hand almost raised as a weapon. When he saw her, his features relaxed a shade. The ladle sank back into the stew as he resumed stirring.

"In the *utility* area," he told her, stretching out the word to carefully pronounce each of its four syllables.

"All of them?" she asked incredulously.

Turning from the industrial stove, Raul picked up

a knife and several carrots he'd peeled earlier. His knife never missed a beat as he created equal-sized pieces. "Yes. They are watching the boiler."

This was less than enlightening. "Watching the boiler do what? Not work?"

The chopping ceased for only a beat. He raised his eyes to hers. "Is new one. It works." The rhythmic sound of knife to board continued.

"We have a new boiler?" she echoed in amazement. Those things cost thousands of dollars. Muriel hadn't been sure, as of last night, that she even had enough money in the fund to buy the boiler a Band-Aid, much less get a new one. "Since when?"

"Since now." Raul looked at his watch, a gift from the shelter when he had been clean and sober for an entire six months. It was his proudest possession. *"A las tres,"* he elaborated.

Three o'clock. Maybe Muriel had gotten in a repairman who'd resurrected the boiler at three, someone who worked on the promise of payment rather than actual cash. But even so, why would everyone be gathered around the boiler? It didn't make any sense.

She needed to see for herself what was going on. "Thanks," she murmured to Raul as she began to head toward the back.

"Is good thing," Raul called after her, craning his neck so that he could be heard.

"Yes, I'm sure it is," Lisa tossed over her shoulder just before she turned the corner and disappeared into the rear of the building.

The utility room also doubled in part as the shelter's laundry room. An overworked, industrial-sized washing machine stood beside an equally large dryer that tended to make a racket ten minutes into its drying process. Both had been donations from the local laundrette when the latter had relinquished its old machines for newer models. The washing machine leaked and the dryer had a tendency to snag clothing, but the shelter was in no position to complain. A gift was a gift.

As a rule, most of the gifts for the shelter had previous owners. But not the boiler.

Raul was right. She could see the box that the boiler had come in discarded to one side. The boiler *was* brand-spanking-new. And, unless she missed her guess, the object of everyone's admiration.

There were so many people there, Lisa found that she had to turn sideways just to get through the crowd, which was gathered around the appliance like pagan worshippers around a newly erected idol.

When she made it to the front, Lisa gestured toward the boiler. Her question went out to anyone who could answer her. "Where did this come from?"

"The truck," Monica piped up eagerly. She

pranced around from toe to toe, the excitement of the group telegraphing itself through her. "I saw it."

Lisa nodded, acknowledging the little girl's response. She tried to look interested, but her mind was elsewhere. She was trying to make sense out of all this.

Looking over Monica's head, her eyes met Muriel's. The director of the shelter looked as if she was in danger of floating away at any moment. She was beaming from ear to ear like a child who had found out that her belief in Santa Claus had been justified after all.

Just where was the money coming from? Lisa's eyes darted over toward Malone, who was holding court in the center of the crowd, then back toward Muriel.

"And who paid for it to be on that truck?" she asked the woman.

Instead of blurting the answer out, Muriel looked directly at Ian. If possible, her face-splitting grin widened even more. "He did."

Lisa heard the words but they didn't quite register. She looked at Malone. "You."

He shrugged, looking, she thought, almost modest, as if all this attention had turned him momentarily shy. As if that were possible. "I got a good deal."

It took a great stretch of her imagination to picture the man shopping around for the large, unwieldy appliance. "On a boiler."

He lifted his shoulders again and let them drop. "Yeah."

She had a hard time believing this. "You went out and just *bought* a boiler."

This time, he moved closer to her. Away from the boiler that the deliverymen had just brought and hooked up. "Well, it really wouldn't fit in my pocket so shoplifting it was kind of out of the question."

A few of the children giggled, but Lisa ignored them. Instead, she motioned for Malone to move over to the side, away from the others who had clearly declared him their king. She was trying to make sense of the man, the motive, the gesture. He was here because he'd been arrested on a DUI, having such little regard for his own life and, incidentally, the lives of anyone who might have crossed his path that he'd gotten behind the wheel and driven while intoxicated. This wasn't the kind of man who acted like the patron saint of homeless shelters.

And yet…

"Why would you do this?" she wanted to know the second they were out of general earshot.

His expression was completely innocent. "Why wouldn't I?"

He was toying with her. "Because it's expensive. Because these people," she lowered her voice even more, "don't *mean* anything to you."

He studied her for a long moment, making her more and more uncomfortable. Making her want to squirm. It was hard for her to return his gaze undaunted. Harder still to keep up the wall she so desperately needed to keep up. Because without it, there was a world of hurt ultimately waiting for her.

She had to focus on that.

"Why is it that you think you know me so well, Kitty? And why is it every time I think we're making progress, you surprise me by making a mad dash back to the beginning of the game board?"

There, he'd said it. Right there in a nutshell, she thought triumphantly. "Exactly for that reason." When he didn't seem to follow her thought, she added, "Because this is a game to you. Because it's all probably a game to you."

But he shook his head, looking calm rather than like someone whose motives had been uncovered.

"Games don't enter into it," he informed her. "It's very simple, really. They needed a boiler," he gestured toward the people who'd been near the boiler. The novelty gone, the excitement leveling off, they were beginning to disperse now. "I have money. Abracadabra: instant solution."

She thought of what the boiler had to cost. Far beyond anything she could have managed without a home loan. "Not so instant for most people." She looked at him for a long moment and then she shook her head, confounded. "I really can't figure you out, Malone."

"There's not much to figure out." Smiling, he

spread out his hands, palms facing upwards. "What you see is what you get."

"Not hardly." He wasn't taking her in for a minute. In the beginning, she would have agreed, but she would have been wrong. She knew that now. "There are a lot of layers to you, Malone."

His eyes held hers, making everyone else in the area disappear. She found that she couldn't look away. "Takes one to know one," he told her quietly.

Before she could say anything more, Muriel came up behind them, as if drawn by the tension that was dancing between her and Malone. Radiating joy, she placed a hand on each of their shoulders. "I say this calls for a celebration." The woman looked from Malone to her. "What do you say?"

"Don't have to convince me," he replied easily, then raised an eyebrow as he looked over toward Lisa. "But Kitty here might need some arm twisting." And with that he followed the others and left the utility room.

Muriel looked at her, puzzled. "Kitty?"

Lisa shrugged dismissively. "Malone seems to take pleasure in corrupting my name."

Muriel laughed softly, obviously enjoying the moment. Lowering her voice even though there was no one else there, she inclined her head and confided, "I don't think that it's your name Mr. Malone would take pleasure in corrupting, dear." Straightening, the woman winked at her.

Lisa blew out a breath. Wasn't going to happen.

Ever. "Whatever." She gave one last look at the boiler. "At least we got a boiler out of this—provided he didn't steal it."

"Oh Lisa, sometimes I fear you are too suspicious for your own good."

And sometimes I'm not suspicious enough.

"Want to grab a cup of coffee?" Ian asked her a couple of hours later as she prepared to leave for the evening.

She was in the hall, about to take her coat out of the closet where she'd left it when he came up behind her. Only the greatest amount of control kept her from sucking in a breath in surprise.

Taking a deep breath, she pulled her hair out from beneath the collar of her jacket. "You'll have to teach me how to do that someday."

Absently, he straightened one side of her collar. He noticed that she stiffened, but she didn't pull away. Pride, he guessed. "Do what?"

She took a discreet step back as she buttoned her jacket. "Materialize out of nowhere."

He looked at her as if he were deadly serious. "It's done with mirrors." And then he smiled. "You were preoccupied. You didn't hear me come up."

He was entirely too observant for her taste. "What are you doing here, anyway?"

He looked at her as if he was trying to make the right guess. "Penance?"

"No, I mean, I didn't see your car in the lot, didn't see Dan waiting for you, so I just thought—"

"That I wasn't here," he guessed. Was she happy or annoyed to find him here, he wondered. He couldn't really read her. But that intrigued him. "I told Dan to take some time for himself while I put in my hours. There's no sense in having him just hang around the parking lot."

"He could come in," she pointed out.

"Why should he have to be put to work when it's my transgression that brought me here?"

She supposed that sounded decent enough, although she really resisted giving him points. Every time she did, she felt the ground beneath her feet slipping and she didn't want to lose her footing—or anything else.

She walked out ahead of him and made her way to the back. Lisa looked around. Malone's car was still nowhere to be seen. "So where's he now?"

Malone looked unperturbed. "He'll be here in half an hour—"

She turned to face him and found that there was much too little space between them. "Is that why you asked me for coffee? Because you have time to kill?"

"That and because I didn't think you'd say yes to dinner," he told her honestly. "Besides, the restaurant down the block looks like they serve passable coffee but you're probably leaving yourself open to food poisoning if you eat there."

The man was definitely not predictable. "You always research things so well?"

The smile went straight into her gut. "It pays to know what you're up against."

She was desperate for a way out of this. Lisa glanced at her watch. "I have to be getting home."

"It's coffee, not dinner and a show," he pointed out. "Fifteen minutes," he promised. "Twenty, tops."

Damn, why were his eyes so haunting? "I'm really not partial to coffee."

"Tea? Diet soda? We could drink water and make paper airplanes out of the napkins."

That made her want to laugh. Maybe there wasn't anything really wrong with that. Laughter was supposed to be good for you. "I never learned how to make paper airplanes."

"Then you're in luck." He was threading his arm through hers, leading her down the block. "I could teach you."

And now she was going along with this. How had that happened? "You don't give up very easily do you?"

"I didn't use to," he admitted.

She didn't see him giving up, *ever.* "And now you do?"

"On some things." He sounded so sincere she thought he was going to release her. But then he flashed that smile of his again. "So it's a yes?"

They were hurrying across the street. "How will Dan find you if we're at the restaurant?"

"I'll drop bread crumbs."

"Don't remember the rest of the fairy tale, do you? The sparrows'll eat them."

"Pebbles then. As far as I know, nothing eats pebbles." He really never missed a beat, did he, she thought.

She laughed, shaking her head. She supposed she really didn't have that much to lose. "Okay, fifteen minutes."

Chapter Nine

She was wrong.

It didn't take Lisa very long to realize that she had a great deal to lose. Mainly, her carefully constructed barriers, erected to protect her from ever getting close to another man, especially Ian Malone. But his considerable charm kept wearing at her foundations. It was difficult putting up a fence around her feelings when the bottom of every slat seemed to be eaten away.

Sitting at the restaurant, listening to Ian talk about nothing and everything, she found herself captivated despite all her efforts not to be. It was as if all the words out of his mouth seemed to weave themselves into one entertaining anecdote or vignette after another.

When he told her about his experience purchasing the shelter's brand-new boiler from a man who hardly spoke English—doing what she assumed was a perfect mimic of the man's accent—and the problems that arose because of the language barrier, she found it difficult not to laugh.

"You know, if I'd been drinking my coffee just now, it would have shot out of my mouth like a sprinkling system left on high," she told him as she tried to suppress a fit of laughter.

"And me without an umbrella." He was grinning, but then he added a little more seriously, "I guess in some ways," his voice grew more quiet, his gaze dwelling on her, "I've always been lucky."

Lisa sincerely doubted that he actually believed that. Not after what he had told her about the earthquake and what had happened to him and to the rest of his family. But the somber thought was hard for her to hang to, at least when he was looking at her like that. As if there was no one else in the crowded restaurant but her. His gaze made her feel all soft inside, as if the very core of her had turned into whipped marshmallow that was melting fast.

For one small second in time—all right, maybe not so small, she allowed—she was tempted to lean over the square table and kiss him. God knew the man looked kissable. In all honesty, she had thought of nothing else since she'd sat down opposite him.

But then she forced herself to sit back, her posture

so ramrod straight it would have brought tears to a drill sergeant's eyes.

"You, um, have a way with words," Lisa finally managed to get out, desperately searching for something to say, to put words between them and this growing wave of desire she was struggling for all she was worth to bank down. She forced her eyes to break contact. She studied the rim of her cup as she asked, "Have you ever thought about becoming a writer?"

This was where he told her what he did for a living, Ian thought. She had just handed him the perfect opening. To not tell her now seemed somehow deceptive and underhanded.

But he really didn't want to give up what he felt he had right now. The protective cloak of anonymity. Because at this moment, Lisa just thought of him as an ordinary man who had perhaps a little too much money in his bank account. Even so, he could see that he was making points with her. And although he'd promised himself that he was never going to get close to another person again, the warmth her presence in his life was generating, the warmth he felt just being around her, surprised him. And he found himself needing that. Wanting that. Just for a little while longer.

And if he told her who he was, that when he *could* write, he wrote as B. D. Brendan, he knew that she would look at him differently. He'd lose the innocence of their relationship. Their association, he mentally corrected himself. He didn't want that to happen, not yet.

God only knew what she might have read in the papers about his other persona. The press liked nothing better than building someone up only to tear them down and since he'd already been built up, he was in the tear-down stage. Ordinarily, that didn't bother him.

But it would if it made her think less of him than she did right now.

So he smiled and shrugged, raising the cup of lukewarm coffee to his lips for another sip before it became stone cold.

"I've thought about writing, yes." Which was the God's honest truth, especially now. Each morning when he rose, the first thing he thought about was writing, wishing he could and still getting nowhere. "But it takes a certain something…"

With a barely audible sigh, he let his voice drift off without finishing the sentence. Just like his manuscript.

"It takes being able to tell stories, entertaining stories," she interjected, thinking of one of her neighbors who, whenever she managed to get an audience, could drone on and on about the latest drama in her life. She could tell stories, all right, but she couldn't entertain. The woman could put hyperactive children to sleep within five minutes, maybe less. "And you really seem to be able to do that." Lisa took a sip of the coffee. "Why don't you think about it?"

"Writing," he repeated. If she only knew the irony in her suggestion.

Lisa nodded. The more she thought about it, the righter it sounded. "Writing."

A grin flashed across his lips. "Okay, I promise I'll think about it." That, Ian mused, was no lie because, with the deadline for his book coming closer and closer, his thoughts, when he wasn't somewhere around this woman, were centered on nothing else.

"That's all anyone can ask," she replied. Lisa set her cup down and looked at him. Was he putting in so much time at the shelter because the people had begun to get to him, or because he wanted to have the experience behind him? If he was like most unwilling "volunteers," it was probably the latter. "You know, at this rate," she continued, watching his expression for some sort of an indication of his true feelings about the shelter, "with you putting in all this extra time, you're going to be finished with all that community service you were sentenced to in a few weeks."

The movement of his shoulders was careless, vague. "I haven't really been keeping track of the time." He had the first week, but then that had faded into the background.

Lisa laughed, shaking her head. "Most people

have it timed down to the exact half second their time is up. They can hardly wait for their community service to be over with."

He had no doubt she was right and he would have numbered among those, except for the fact that of late, he was beginning to feel that maybe life wasn't so pointless, maybe there was a reason for things, specifically for his existence, just as she'd suggested that time when he'd first told her about his family. He liked the quick smile he received from the kids at the shelter when he did something for them, liked the feeling of doing something, however small, that mattered.

"Yeah, well, maybe that's because they probably have busy lives to get back to." He looked at her, considering what he had just said. "All except for you. Your life's busy and yet you still keep coming back. Why? When you don't have to."

He was wrong there, she thought. She had to come back. If she didn't, she felt as if something was lacking in her life. "I like helping. These people at the shelter, they have so little. Sometimes it makes me almost feel guilty that I have so much."

So much. Her words echoed in his head. It was all relative, he thought. "I thought you were a teacher."

"I am." She knew what he was getting at, but her life was full even without material things. "But I have my own house, I can provide for my son…" She stopped abruptly, mystified. "How did this turn around to be about me?"

Ian leaned over the table, smiling at her, his eyes pulling her to him. "Maybe it is. Maybe it's always been about you."

She had no idea what he was saying, only that she could almost feel his words, soft-spoken and velvety, caressing her. Coaxing her to lean in closer to him. Before she realized it, she *was* leaning over the table again, her posture fluid.

As he watched her, her breath caught in her throat. In a noisy third-rate restaurant, with unintelligible music playing in the background adding to the din, Ian gently cupped her cheek with his hand. He lifted her head up just a fraction.

And then he kissed her.

It was a soft, sensual kiss, a delicate meeting of lips upon lips.

And yet, inside of her the commotion could have only been equaled to the kind of activity that explodes in a Las Vegas casino when someone hits a jackpot on a slot machine. Lights, sirens and cheering went off, vibrating in her head, in her chest. She was hardly conscious of rising from her seat slightly. The next moment, she'd thrown herself full bore into the kiss.

The more it deepened, the harder her heart pounded. The more her head spun.

Ian buried his hands in her hair, his fingers molding around her head, holding her in place. He wasn't supposed to be doing this, wasn't supposed to be hitting on this woman. It would make things awkward at the shelter to say the least. He hit on models, on the scores of self-centered women he came across in his walk of life. Beautiful, self-absorbed, shallow women who were good in bed and forgettable three feet away from it.

Choosing them and only them to make love with was the best way he knew how to survive—how not to get caught up in the intricate delicacies of a relationship. The best way he knew how not to have his heart ripped out of his chest without the benefit of an anesthetic.

But oh, God, he did enjoy this, enjoyed kissing this woman. It was addictive even before the first contact was made, just as he knew it would be. Mentally, he'd already been here. Imagined what kissing her would be like, what making love with her would be like. But he had convinced himself that the fantasy would be better than the reality. For him, that was always the case.

This time, it was different.

Kissing Lisa was every bit as arousing, as stimulating, as head spinning as he'd imagined it would be.

And more.

And that worried him.

Worried him because this kiss didn't mark the end of his temptation. It was just the beginning. And now he was left to wonder….Wonder what the rest of it would be like. What being with her in the full sense of the word would be like.

Somewhere in the far reaches of a nether world, someone was nervously clearing his throat. "Um, Mr. Malone, I could come back."

The uncertain voice of his driver broke through the haze that had overtaken Ian's brain. Served him right for calling Dan to tell him where he was.

It took Ian a moment to clear his head, to search for and find the composure that had been completely dismantled and was now in serious jeopardy of being burnt to a crisp.

"What?" he finally managed, drawing back from Lisa who had pulled herself away from him as if her upper torso was mounted on some sort of spring-action device.

"I could come back. I mean if you're busy, and you look like you are, I could come back," Dan repeated lamely. "Drive around the block or just park somewhere until you're ready…" His voice drifted off as he shifted from foot to foot, looking as if he wished he'd looked in through the plateglass window before venturing into the restaurant.

Lowering her eyes to avoid the driver's, Lisa looked at her watch. "Oh God, look at the time," she cried suddenly. It wasn't fifteen minutes later, or even thirty minutes later. It was almost an hour later than she'd originally promised Casey she'd be home. Lisa was out of the booth and on her feet like a shot.

"I've got to be getting home. I'll see you," she mumbled, tossing the phrase into the air as she looked straight ahead. "Thanks for the coffee."

And then she was gone.

There was a hangdog expression on the large, affable man's face. "I'm really sorry, Mr. Malone," Dan apologized as if he expected to be tongue-lashed for his untimely entrance. "I didn't mean to ruin anything for you."

Ian took a deep breath. That had been close. Any longer and he might have been a goner.

Rising, he took out his wallet and placed several bills down, more than enough to cover the two coffees as well as an inordinately large tip. He slipped his wallet back into his jacket and began heading for the door. "Oh, on the contrary, Dan, you came just in time to rescue me."

Lengthening his stride, Dan fell into step right beside his employer. Puzzled, he scratched his head as he tried to absorb what he was hearing and reconcile it with what he'd witnessed.

"You didn't look like a man who needed rescuing to me." Moving ahead, he managed to open the door in time for Ian.

Once outside the restaurant, Ian paused. The night was cool, crisp. The air was moist with the promise of the rain that was to come. He liked this kind of weather, almost more than the warm, sunny days that California was known for. He wished the rest of him could cool off as quickly as the day had.

Ian looked across the street toward the shelter that stood in the center of the block. She had left for the night, he reminded himself, drawing his jacket in closer to him. Times like this, he missed smoking. Missed having something to do with his hands, something to divert his thoughts.

"Trust me, Dan," he said, half to himself and half to the man at his elbow. "I did. And I do."

Dan shook his head. It was obvious that he just didn't follow that line of thinking. But he knew better than to question. That wasn't what he was being paid for and the money was good, not to mention the fringe benefits. His wife had raved for days about the chocolate he'd brought home on Halloween.

A half smile curved Ian's lips. He knew Dan probably thought he was crazy.

Maybe he was.

In the circles he usually traveled, he was known as a daredevil, someone who took uncalculated risks, who did insane things. Someone who dared Death to come and find him. It wasn't hard when you didn't care if you lived or died.

But in this one area in his life, in the area where it meant that he could be risking his heart, his feelings, the very essence of the things that made him who he was, Ian was determined to play it safe.

Not an easy thing to do, he thought, when he'd just succeeded in voluntarily burning away his safety net.

The moment she had the key in the lock and opened the door, she saw her mother rising from the sofa, her small shoulder bag clutched in her hand.

Susan Kittridge was wearing her security guard uniform. The midnight-blue fabric was reminiscent of the uniform she'd so proudly worn for twenty-three years. Instead of soothing her, it reminded her how much she missed being on the force.

She lost no time in crossing to her daughter, disappointment in her eyes. "I had to get Chris Hollis to take over part of my shift."

Lisa knew it would do no good to offer to reimburse her for that. Her mother wouldn't take her money, so there was no buying her off and securing a little leeway. "I'm sorry, Mom." She pulled off her jacket and hung it up, then stepped out of her shoes. "I lost track of the time."

Susan sighed, shaking her head. It was hard upbraiding a daughter whose sin was giving too much of herself to people who had nothing. But, she reminded herself, Lisa's first duty was to her son, to make sure that Casey wouldn't get shortchanged because his mother was spreading herself too thin.

"Obviously." Susan frowned slightly. "He's upstairs, still awake and waiting for you if I know my grandson." Susan took her jacket off the same rack that Lisa has just hung up hers. "I'm going to go in and relieve—" Susan stopped dead. The faint hint of color and blurred lip outline on Lisa's mouth caught her attention. "Lisa," her eyes narrowed, "what happened to your lipstick?" she wanted to know.

Lisa turned her head to the side, away from her mother's scrutinizing look. "Nothing," she murmured. "Why?"

Susan shifted in order to get a better look. "Because it's blurred."

Lisa moved her head the other way, pretending to look for something in her jacket. Damn it, why had she been in such a hurry to get home? Why hadn't she looked into a mirror before she walked in? She knew what her mother was like these days—a frustrated crime scene investigator in waiting.

"Lipstick fades, Mom." She shrugged carelessly. "None of these tubes last—"

Susan brought an abrupt halt to the excuse by catching her daughter's chin in her hand, forcing Lisa to turn her head in her direction.

"I know the difference between faded and smudged, Lisa. I'm not a hundred years old with failing eyesight." As she spoke, Susan examined the evidence more closely. "You kissed someone."

Lisa pulled her head away and took a step back. "No."

Twenty-three years on the force had taught her when to be flexible. She rephrased her assumption. "Someone kissed you."

The answer to that was yes, but if she admitted as much, there would be no end to the questions that would come pouring out of her mother. So she lied for the sake of peace. "No."

Susan was always on point. "So, a dog got fresh with you?"

Lisa sighed, shaking her head. She didn't remember being put through this kind of questioning when she was a teenager coming home from a date. Why now?

"You really did retire much too soon from the precinct, Mom."

"Not by choice," Susan reminded her. If she had her way, she'd still be on the street, bagging the bad guys. "This isn't an interrogation, Lisa, this is your mother, asking a question."

She knew her mother meant well, but being asked still annoyed her. "I'm over eighteen, Mom."

To her surprise, her mother nodded and said, "Which is why I'm concerned that you don't look like this more often. Excuse me," she corrected herself, "more than once." Her mother gave her what Lisa knew was her most penetrating gaze. "Now, were you the victim of a drive-by kissing or does this person who kissed you have a name?"

Lisa waved her hand dismissively. She didn't

want to talk about it right now. Maybe never. "It's nothing, Mom."

"If it's nothing, you can tell me." Susan said it so persuasively, she almost managed to convince her. Even with her head turned, Lisa could feel her mother's eyes on her. "You know me, I'm not about to stop until—"

She shut her eyes, sighing. "It's that guy that the court sent over to do some community service. Ian."

Susan nodded. She knew exactly who her daughter was talking about. "The cute one."

Lisa swung around to look at her mother. "I didn't say that," she protested.

There was a knowing expression on her mother's face. "You didn't have to. It's written all over you." Smiling, Susan reached up and squeezed her shoulder. "Good for you, Lisa."

Lisa sighed, exasperated. "Nothing happened, Mother," she insisted. "We went out for coffee."

"Coffee and a kiss. Good start."

"Mommy!" The small voice somehow managed to project all the way down the stairs.

"That would be your son," Susan told her. She nodded up toward the stairs. "Go say hello before he forgets what you look like." And then she dealt her ace. "Unless you'd rather stay here and give me details."

Lisa didn't need any more incentive than that. Turning on her heel she was moving up the stairs at an incredible speed considering how tired she'd been when she walked in through the door a few minutes ago.

"Coming, Casey."

Chapter Ten

Lisa decided to cut back on her hours at the shelter, at least temporarily.

With Thanksgiving now just a few days away, she was literally swamped. There were preparations to be made both at home and in her classroom, so she let things slide at the shelter more than she knew she should. But it couldn't be helped, she was even too busy to breathe regularly.

At least, that was the excuse she gave herself. By not showing up at the shelter, it also meant not running into Malone.

The truth was, she still hadn't fully processed what had happened between them at the restaurant.

If she even actually understood what had happened. There were a myriad of feelings and emotions that had been unleashed with that one simple kiss. Feelings and emotions she didn't want unleashed.

All she knew was that it scared her.

Because if she had been feeling vulnerable before, now it felt as if she were spread across a sacrificial altar, each wrist and ankle bound to one of the four corners. There was no way for her to move to escape whatever it was that was coming.

Unless she didn't show up at all.

So she decorated, baked and planned menus—and stayed far away. Rather than donate what free time she had to Providence Shelter, she stayed after school to tutor several children in her class who somehow seemed to have gotten through second grade without being able to read a single word.

But doing so made her think of Monica. Monica and the book Casey had donated to the cause of helping the little girl learn to read. She'd turned out to be incredibly smart, incredibly eager and a dream to teach. All she had needed was someone to show interest, someone to start her off. She'd done that. And then Malone had taken over where she'd left off.

She didn't want to dwell on his nicer qualities. It made her yearn, and yearning was a bad thing.

Since it was the Tuesday before Thanksgiving, only one of the three children she was working with was able to remain after class. The other two had already begun an early vacation with their parents.

Jamie Grainger sat at his desk, concentrating so hard on the open book in front of him, it was as if every bone in his body were rigidly focused. All except for his left foot, which he kept swinging back and forth beneath his desk.

He was short for his age. Short and delicate looking. But there was something about the boy, a light in his blue eyes that told Lisa not to give up on him.

At times, that wasn't easy. He seemed to have a harder time of it than the other two and it took more effort to get through to him. But she was determined that he was going to read as well as, if not better than, the other children in her class.

Rather than sit at her desk the way she did when she had all three students after school, Lisa had pulled up a chair next to Jamie. It was an effort on her part to make the learning experience less threatening and more of an intimate experience for him.

They'd been at it for more than an hour and her throat felt raspy and parched since she'd been the one doing most of the sounding out.

"I'll be right back," Lisa promised as she got up from her seat to get a drink of water. She patted his shoulder much the same way she did Casey's when she was encouraging him. "You stay here and keep at it."

The dark head bobbed up and down, resigned. Jamie gathered the book in closer, sighed audibly and started trying to sound out the sentence they had already gone over twice.

Lisa pressed her lips together. She had no doubt that it was a frustrating experience. For both of them, she thought, looking at the boy over her shoulder as she left the classroom.

It wasn't just her throat that felt as if it had gone dry, it was her energy level as well. She was very close to running on empty. Lisa paused over the water fountain located just outside the girl's bathroom and drank in deeply.

There were times when she felt like a cheerleader in a cemetery, unable to arouse any enthusiasm, not even so much as a thimbleful. But there were other times, she reminded herself, when the exact opposite was true. She was just slipping into the holiday blues.

Snap out of it. You've got a great job, a great kid, lots to be thankful for.

Lisa ducked into the bathroom. Throwing some cold water in her face, she looked at her reflection in the mirror and gave herself a not-so-silent pep talk about not being such a wuss.

Revived, she quickly left the bathroom and walked back down the hall to her classroom. She'd taken exactly one step across the threshold when she came to a dead stop.

Jamie was no longer alone. There was someone sitting in the chair that she had been in a few minutes ago.

Ian.

Ian was talking to Jamie as if they had always known each other. Warm, friendly, and he was actually helping the boy read by sounding out the words.

"Okay, you know this one, we just did it. Now what's this sound? Do you remember?" Ian silently went through the motions, mouthing the sound.

Jamie watched his mouth intently, then made a noise as if he was blowing the letter "F" over his lower lip. Ian grinned as if the boy had single-handedly won the international little league championship.

"Fantastic. And now what word do the last three letters make?" As a hint, he flexed his upper arm and then pointed to it.

Jamie's eyes were as large as saucers. "Arm!" he announced with glee.

"Arm it is. Now, sound it out, Jamie. Put that together. You can do it," he encouraged. "What's the word?"

"F-arm. F-arm." A light bulb suddenly went off over his head. "Farm!" Jamie declared.

Ian beamed, caught up in the experience. "Right on, Tiger. Now you're rolling. Okay, what's this word? Just because it's big doesn't mean you can't break it down to bite-sized pieces."

"I like bite-sized pieces," Jamie told him.

Ian ruffled his hair. "Me, too."

For a few moments, Lisa hung back, watching, listening, completely fascinated. She'd seen him with the children at the shelter, but this was something new, something over and above his normal behavior. This was real patience.

Which was the real Ian Malone? The laid-back flirt? The careless man who drove under the influence without regard for his own life? The incredibly generous man who thought nothing of shelling out his own money to improve the lot of people he hardly knew? Or this one—a gentle, patient man teaching a restless, shy boy burdened with a stutter how to read.

He wasn't stuttering, she suddenly realized.

Jamie had hesitated when he was sounding words out, but he hadn't stuttered. Not once. Not for Ian the way he did around her and everyone else.

She stared at Ian with renewed interest and curiosity, doing her best to push any personal feelings aside. Who *was* this man?

She wasn't going to solve that this afternoon. And it was time to take back her classroom and her student, she thought, coming forward. "What are you doing here?" she asked Ian.

He looked up as if he'd known all along that she was in the doorway, observing him. His smile was easy and all the more unsettling for its assumptions. "Helping Jamie nail down some lines."

Actors talk like that, she thought. Was that what Ian was, an out of work actor? There were times when he looked vaguely familiar to her, but she'd chalked that up to the fact that she interacted with a lot of people in her line of work.

But if he was an actor, maybe she'd seen him in something.

That wasn't important, she upbraided herself. What was important here was Jamie.

She turned her attention to him. "You did very well, Jamie. I think you can go home now." She crossed to the window and looked out. "Your mom's waiting for you in the parking lot," she verified.

Jamie didn't need any more convincing. He was on his feet in an instant. "Okay. Thanks." He looked at the man to his right and grinned broadly. "Bye now."

"See you around, Tiger." Ian waited until the boy had left the classroom before turning toward her. "Jamie's slightly dyslexic," he told her. "That's probably why he has so much trouble."

She already knew that, but she was trained to pick up on that sort of thing. "How would you know that?" And then the answer to her question came to her. "You're dyslexic, too, aren't you?"

Rather than look evasive, he smiled at her. "Nothing gets by you, does it, Kitty? I'm not as bad as some, but yes, I am slightly dyslexic."

He wasn't the type to allow any kind of shortcoming to get in his way. He had a way of toughing things out. She had no idea how she knew, she just did. But there was something else she still wanted the answer to.

"How did you find me?" She'd never told him where she taught. How had he managed to come to the right school.

"Muriel," he told her.

She sighed. It figured. The woman was more than a little smitten with him. Muriel would have thought nothing of giving out her place of work to a smooth talker like Ian, especially after the boiler bequest. "Muriel talks too much."

"She's a charming woman," he countered, although not disputing her assessment.

Lisa made no comment. Something else was bothering her. How had Malone managed to just walk into the elementary school, especially after hours? Schools had changed in the last dozen years. Precautions were taken as a matter of course. People couldn't just come and go as they pleased. There were safeguards against that.

"How did you get in here, anyway? We have a security guard on the grounds."

They did and he had run into the man. The guard, a big, strapping red-faced young man barely out of his teens had challenged his presence on the premises. But before he could tell the guard who he was looking for, the man had recognized him from his picture on the back of his last book.

As it turned out, the guard was an avid fan of science fiction.

He'd given the guard his autograph in exchange for his silence, explaining that he didn't want anyone else knowing he had stopped by the school. The guard had been pleased to be taken into his confidence and had promised, almost eagerly, not to say a word to anyone.

Ian shrugged carelessly. "I guess he didn't think I was dangerous."

"A lot he knows," she murmured under her breath, thinking of the other night at the restaurant.

He smiled, making himself at home on the edge of her desk. "Do you think I'm dangerous, Kitty?"

Oh God, yes, she thought.

If she didn't feel that there was something dangerous about him, her adrenaline wouldn't insist on jacking up every time Malone was anywhere in the vicinity. But saying as much somehow sounded incredibly juvenile, so she merely shrugged.

"Let's just say that I don't think you're mild-mannered Clark Kent and leave it at that."

He grinned. "Very flattering."

Nope, this was not the way to go, Lisa decided. She needed to be the one in control here. Otherwise, things might get out of hand, the way they clearly had at the restaurant.

The second she thought of the restaurant, she could swear she felt her lips growing sensitive. An ache was suddenly born in the very core of her.

Just a normal physical reaction, she silently insisted. She hadn't made love with a man since, well, since before Casey was born. She'd never believed in having casual relationships or flings. Matt had been the one love of her life. Her first lover. And her only lover.

But it was only natural to have these tingling sensations, she told herself, these longings.

Desperate for a subject where she had the upper hand, she heard herself asking, "Do you have plans for Thanksgiving?"

His plans involved escape, but he knew better than to phrase it that way. "I generally go away for the holidays. Why?" He looked at her, curious. "Are you inviting me over?"

Well, this was certainly awkward, she thought. She hadn't meant to give him the wrong impression. "Um, I was hoping to get you to come and help feed the people at the shelter Thanksgiving Day. Most people spend the day with their families and I thought—"

It wasn't hard to figure out what she thought. "—that since I didn't have one and needed to redeem myself, I'd be the perfect candidate."

The way he said it made her feel guilty, as if she were saying that he didn't count. She lifted one shoulder, then let it drop self-consciously. "Something like that."

It was on the tip of his tongue to refuse. But then,

if he refused, he would be somewhere watching people enjoy themselves, instead of at a facility where the people had all shared in some misfortune or other. People he could identify with.

"Sure," he said, surprising himself as much as her. "Why not? What time would you want me there?"

God, that was easy. Almost too easy. The information dribbled from her lips as if preprogrammed.

"Preparations start at eight in the morning. That's when Raul begins to get the turkeys ready for the ovens. If you just want to help serve and not cook, you need to be at the shelter by noon."

"Noon," he repeated. "Or eight. Okay, I got it." He shifted a tad closer to her. "Now can we talk?"

She felt her space invaded, but to push back from her chair would be a sign of weakness. So she continued sitting where she was, feeling nervous.

"About?" she heard herself asking.

His eyes held hers. "About why you haven't shown up at the shelter since I kissed you."

She was drowning in an open sea. "You have nothing to do with it."

He knew he'd caught her and he wasn't about to let her go. "Convince me."

She took a breath, her shoulders stiffening. "You think a lot of yourself, don't you?"

"On the contrary, I don't think of myself at all. What I do find myself thinking of—quite against my will—" he admitted, lowering his voice to almost a whisper, "is you."

Damn but he was good. "I didn't think that was possible."

"What?" His smile wove its way under her skin. Making her not just warm but close to broiling. "Thinking about you?"

"No, being insulting and flattering in the same sentence."

Ian's mouth curved. She was a challenge. He'd always loved a challenge, even though he knew that this time he should be backing off. More than that, he should be running for cover. But her mouth was too sweet and her eyes were too compelling, so he stayed where he was and played the hand that was dealt him. Wondering where it would end.

"I have a gift." He took her hand in his. Her fingertips were icy, but he made no mention of it. "God's honest truth, Kitty, I am as reluctant as you to get into anything, but there was a definite connection last Wednesday. When we kissed—"

"When you kissed me," she corrected.

He inclined his head. If she needed to believe that, far be it from him to take that away from her. "If it makes you feel any better," he allowed, starting again. "When I kissed you, there were definite sparks going off."

She took offense at his phrasing. Was he patronizing her? "What do you mean if it makes me feel any better? That's what happened. You kissed me."

His smile infuriated her. She decided to cling to that reaction. It kept her from melting. "You're ignoring the important part."

"Which is?" she challenged.

"That you kissed me back. And that there *were* sparks."

She blew out a breath. It had never been in her to lie. But this was her self-preservation they were talking about. If she gave in, if she admitted that he had her reacting the way he did, she was opening herself up to plunging down a very slippery slope.

Lisa ran her tongue along her lower lip. "I'm not going to deny that you're an attractive man—"

"Attractive is for department store dummies and runway models who are just as empty-headed and hollow. We're not talking about *attractive,* Kitty, we're talking about a definite connection being made here. We're talking about chemistry—"

She shook her head. "No, no chemistry," she insisted. "In my experience, when there's chemistry, things are in danger of blowing up."

"Not always," he countered. "Look, Kitty, I don't exactly know what's happening here or where it's coming from or where it's going to go. Most likely nowhere," he guessed philosophically. "But I think we owe it to ourselves as explorers to—explore."

He made it sound like a hike in the park. But it

was so much more than that, with all kinds of emotional pitfalls. "I'm not an explorer, Malone. I'm a mother, a teacher, sometimes a daughter. But nowhere in that definition of me does the word *explorer* even remotely come up."

Undaunted, he grinned, creating a small tidal wave in her belly. "Where's your sense of adventure?"

"See above," she countered. "It's all wrapped up in the aforementioned three things. I've used up my entire supply of sense of adventure being all those other things."

"What about you, the woman?" he wanted to know.

She looked away. It was time for her to be leaving. Her excuse for being here had just walked out to meet his mother. She pulled her purse out of the bottom drawer of her desk. "Canceled for lack of interest."

He laughed shortly. Not from where he was standing. "On whose part?"

She slammed the drawer shut so hard, it vibrated the rest of the desk. "Look, Malone, get this through your head. I am not interested in having an affair."

"Never liked that word. Too cheap-sounding. How about a relationship?" he suggested. "Or a romance? Or an interlude? Any of those words strike your fancy?"

Why was he backing her into a corner? Was he going to chip away at her until she said yes? Because she wanted to say yes. It was just that she knew what was going to happen to her once this was over. It would have too much of an impact on her. She couldn't do things by half measures and once he was gone, she'd fall to pieces.

"You can't just define things with words," she insisted.

He looked as if he was disappointed in her. "You as a teacher should know better than that, Kitty. All we have are words."

She tried again, although why she didn't just pick up and leave was beyond her. "I mean that feelings don't fit neatly into carefully carved niches—"

He stopped her right there. "So you have feelings for me?"

She struggled with exasperation. "I was just giving you an example." She sighed, her teeth sinking into her bottom lip to keep from saying something she would regret. "Did you come here to give me a hard time?" she wanted to know.

"No," he said slowly. "I came here because I missed you. Because I wanted to make sure you were all right and because I didn't want you to get the wrong idea about what happened."

Okay, she'd bite. "And just what is the right idea about what happened?"

She'd never seen so much mischief in one person's eyes as she did in his at that moment. "*Carpe diem* comes to mind."

"Seize the day?" she echoed incredulously.

He touched her cheek lightly, his fingers barely skimming along the surface. Exciting them both. "That's the phrase," he whispered.

And the next moment, he gave in to his inclinations and seized the day.

Chapter Eleven

*B*etter.

This was even better.

The thought telegraphed itself through Ian's mind the second he began to kiss her. This kiss was even better than the one they'd shared the other evening.

Without a table between them acting as a barrier, he was able to have more contact and Ian took full advantage of that. He drew Lisa closer to him and wrapped his arms around her. Holding her against him so that the soft, subtle nuances of her body were fitted against him, fueling the tension, the excitement that was stirring and growing within.

To add to that, he could feel Lisa's heart racing against his chest, racing just as fast as his heart was. It was only a matter of time before they would make love together. It was a given.

He didn't know if that thrilled him or scared the hell out of him.

Probably both and almost in equal shares.

She didn't want the kiss, the surge it created. Threading her arms around Ian's neck, she ached to have this continued and yet she knew it couldn't. It had to stop.

Now.

For one thing, a student or, more likely, a teacher, could pass by and look in. And then what? This was a compromising situation at best. Rumors of inappropriate behavior had begun with far less.

And for another and, far more important a reason, if she continued to be submerged in this all-consuming kiss, she was going to want more.

She *already* wanted more and that was simply out of the question.

Even though every fiber of her body had begun to beg for it.

So Lisa placed her hands against his chest and pushed him back, though not with as much force as she was capable of exuding and maybe with more than a touch of lamented reluctance.

She drew a long breath in before saying anything. It would come across better if her voice didn't squeak when she spoke. "Are you going to apologize for that, too?"

"Hell, no." He smiled into her eyes, focusing on how much he'd just enjoyed that. "That would be like apologizing for being present at the performance of a miracle."

Amusement highlighted her face. "Does that line usually work?"

"I have no idea," he told her honestly. "It's not a line and I've never said it before. Because I've never felt it before." He paused to take in air, not bothering to hide the fact that she pretty well had left him breathless. "You do pack quite a wallop, Kitty."

She'd ceased to mind the nickname. For a woman who was completely agitated inside, she was feeling pretty mellow. "You should see my right cross."

Her comeback made him laugh. "I bet it's really something." He didn't bother to consider his next words. Maybe it was better that way. There was such a thing as overthinking. "Would you like to go out to dinner with me?"

"Yes." The answer rushed out, but then she added, "But I won't."

Were they back at that damned first square again? "Why not?"

"Because we shouldn't be getting involved."

Ian ran a fingertip ever so lightly along her lips. The unguarded look in her eyes, the burst of sensual excitement he saw there, telegraphed itself all through him, putting him on high alert.

"I think," he put forth, "the *getting* part is really a moot point, Kitty. I'd say that we're already there."

Lisa let out a ragged breath. The man was right. But forewarned was forearmed, right? She could definitely put the skids on before it became a toboggan ride down a steep slope. Moreover, she could approach the situation like a sensible adult. After all, she wasn't some mindless teenager—no matter how much that kiss had scrambled all her systems. She had the benefit of experience and maturity on her side.

"All right," Lisa agreed. "Dinner."

The smile that bloomed on his face made the whole thing worth it. "Great, I'll pick you up—"

"My house," she interjected quickly.

It was part of her hastily conceived plan to save herself before it became too late. The sad fact of life was that nothing cooled a man's jets faster than meeting a woman's son—unless it was meeting a woman's son *and* meeting her mother, then discovering that both lived with her. It would deftly take the matter out of her hands and swiftly put an end to whatever it was that she was secretly nursing along.

Getting involved was not a good thing. She *knew* that. It had taken her all this time to recover from losing Matt and, even so, there were times when she missed him so much she thought her heart was going to break into a million little pieces. She couldn't set herself up to revisit pain like that again just because her hormones had decided to go on a holiday.

Ian looked at her for a long moment, mulling over what Lisa had just proposed. "You want to cook for me?" he said slowly, as if to verify what he'd thought he heard.

The way he said it brought an amused smile to her lips. "Afraid?"

"Intrigued," he countered. "I don't think I've ever had a woman cook for me before." He thought for a moment. "No, never," he decided.

That was because he just wasn't the homebody type. Not to mention that he'd probably never stayed with any one woman long enough to have her try out her culinary skills on him. That just proved that she was right. Even if she was in the market for someone in her life, Ian Malone wouldn't be the one for her. He wouldn't qualify.

"Never have a relationship last long enough?" she guessed.

No, he hadn't. And that was by design. But even if there actually had been a relationship to look back on, none of the women he'd ever been with actually knew where the stove was located, much less what to do with it once it was found. He supposed Lisa would have called them bimbos, or something worse.

On second thought, he decided, Lisa wasn't the type. She wasn't catty or vindictive when it came to other women the way some were. In the weeks that he had been around her, the only thing he had come away with was how kind she was to other people.

Still, there was no reason to go into his past or the lack of any actual relationships that lasted more than ten days. "No." And then he asked, "What time would you like me over tonight?"

"Seven." Any later and Casey would be in bed and it was important for him to be there. But it gave her a little less than three hours to get ready.

Lisa's head began scrambling as she threw together a menu in her mind.

He'd wanted to take her out, to impress her a little, but he wasn't about to make her think this was a power struggle about who called the shots. This was a very fragile thing he was working with.

"Seven it is."

The smile on his face, so sensual, so sexual, had her recalculating everything. It suddenly hit her that Malone might be getting the wrong idea here. That he might see the invitation as a prelude to a night of lovemaking, especially after the intensity of that kiss. She needed to set him straight right at the beginning. And then the ball would be in his court.

"By the way, there'll be four of us."

She was being cautious, he thought. "Another couple?" he guessed.

She laughed. "Only if you consider my son and my mother a couple."

Had he heard her wrong? "Your mother?"

She nodded. "She lives with me. She helps me take care of Casey while I'm working or at the shelter. My mother's an ex-cop."

Ian grinned. He had the definite impression that she was telling him all this for a reason. "Are you warning me, Kitty?"

She pulled back her shoulders. "Just thought you'd want to have all the facts before you came over."

She was trying to get him to beg off. *No such luck, Kitty.* He had his foot in the door and he was about to wedge it open. "Kitty, to be allowed to enter the inner sanctum, I'd brave an entire regiment of cops, even if they were all related to you."

The tips of her fingers began to tingle. Oh God, what had she just gone and let herself in for?

"All right then," she said, her mouth suddenly devoid of any saliva. "Seven."

"Seven," he echoed as he walked out.

Two and a half hours later, the tips of her fingers were no longer tingling. They had turned into icicles and most of the feeling seemed to have gone out of them. When she dropped the large spoon she'd been stirring with—after dropping several other things before that—her mother gave her an inquisitive glance.

"You all right, Lisa?"

Lisa wiped her hands on her apron, wishing there was a way to flatten the butterflies that had taken up residence just beneath it.

"No, I'm not all right," she admitted, frustrated. "I'm an idiot."

Susan paused to turn one of the hoops that had caught in her daugher's hair forward. She merely smiled as Lisa pulled her head back. "Well, since in your case it's not a congenital condition, I think there might be hope for you. Why are you an idiot?"

Lisa blew the tips of her bangs back, out of her eyes. "Because I invited Ian over."

Susan knew better than to try to finish the job for her daughter. She kept her hands at her sides. "That doesn't make you an idiot, dear, that makes you semi-normal. I was beginning to think I'd given birth to a closet nun."

Lisa discovered that she had only about half a drop of patience left. "It's dinner, Mom, not an orgy."

Her mother patted her face, giving her a maddening look. "One can only hope."

Exasperation broke through thinly constructed restraints. "Mo-ther."

Susan raised an eyebrow, more in amusement than in annoyance. "Don't take that tone with me, Lisa Anne Kittridge. You're a healthy, red-blooded young woman—well, fairly young," she amended, trying to goad her daughter. "And I want more grand-children. You did such a great job with Casey, think what you could do now that you've gone past the learning curve."

Walking out of the kitchen into the living room, Lisa threw up her hands. "I'm having a nervous breakdown and you're trying to turn me into a baby machine."

Her mother studied her face. "If you're having a nervous breakdown, this guy must really be hot stuff."

Lisa had begun pacing, bunching her hands up in the pockets of her apron and clenching and un-clenching them. "I don't know why I'm doing this. I was happy. I *am* happy," she declared defensively, swinging around on her heel so that she faced her mother. And then she began pacing again. "I don't need some man to come waltzing in and validate my existence."

"Nothing wrong with a little validation every now and then." Turning, Susan looked out the window and saw someone coming up the walk. The man was gorgeous, she thought. If he was half as nice as he looked, Lisa had hit the jackpot. All she could think was that it was about time. "Especially when it looks like that." She looked back at her daughter in amaze-ment. "You didn't tell me he was gorgeous."

Gorgeous. She supposed he was that. But it still didn't change the fact that this was all wrong, that it shouldn't be happening.

"You didn't ask," she said hoarsely.

Susan took it in stride. "I'll put it on my list of interrogation questions," she promised, looking back through the window again. The man was almost at the front door. "You sure you don't want me to whisk Casey away to McDonald's—or better yet, take both of us over to Frank's house for the evening?"

Subtlety had never been her mother's thing, Lisa thought, irritated. "Why don't you just put me up on a block with a price tag tied to my toe?"

Susan paused as if to consider the option. "I hadn't thought of that."

God, but she felt like screaming, "Mother!"

Susan lightly squeezed the tip of her daughter's chin just as the doorbell rang. Melodic chimes resounded throughout the house. "Smile pretty, honey. Your date is here."

Lisa clenched her teeth together in addition to her hands. "He's not my date."

"Okay," Susan said agreeably, "your would-be lover's here."

Lisa closed her eyes. Her mother was going to embarrass her, she just knew it. What was worse, she was going to do it intentionally. "Mother!"

"Lower your voice, Lisa. Men don't like their women to be screechy." With that, she turned the doorknob and opened the front door. She smiled warmly at the man on her doorstep. A vague sense of recognition wafted through her, but she couldn't place where she knew him from. "Hello, I'm Susan, Lisa's mother. Have we met before?"

Damn, did the woman recognize him? "Not that I know of," he replied easily, keeping his smile in place. The older woman resembled her daughter. They had the same dark hair, the same electric liquid-green eyes, the same slender, athletic build. And the same handshake. Firm, strong, unafraid of judgment. He took an instant liking to the woman. "You're the ex-policewoman."

Susan raised her hands as if in surrender. "No guns tonight, I promise." Just then, drawn by voices, her grandson entered the living room. "Casey, c'mon, you'll be late."

Casey looked at her, his small eyebrows drawing together in confusion. "Late for what?"

Susan cast one long look at the man who had just come in before telling her grandson, "The rest of your life."

Panic made a direct hit to the pit of Lisa's stomach. "She's just kidding," she told first Casey, then Ian. She shot her mother a withering look that was meant to glue Susan Kittridge in place. "She's staying."

Susan never gave up easily. "I haven't seen my son Frank in a while," she told Ian. "I thought tonight might be a good night to bond with him."

There were definite signals being sent here. Signals crossing signals. And Ian had a hunch that he was both the cause and caught in the crossfire.

"Please don't leave on my account," he said to Susan.

Susan exchanged glances with her daughter, the look on the older woman's face saying that she liked this man already.

Then you take him, Mom, Lisa thought in frustration. God knew her mother was far better suited to Malone than she was.

"My mother is staying," Lisa declared in a voice that was not to be argued with as she held her hand out for Ian's jacket. He quickly shed it and handed it to her. "She's the entertainment portion of our evening." With short, quick steps, she went to the hall closet, opened the door, hung up the jacket and placed her mother's purse on a hook before closing the door again. Firmly. "Tell him about some of the cases you've had, Mom." One hand on her hip, the other still on the doorknob, she looked at her mother pointedly. "The ones that didn't involve justifiable homicide."

Ian felt a tug on the lower edge of his pullover. When he looked down, he saw that the boy had crossed over to him and was now standing by his side, his small, oval face upturned. "Who are you?"

He squatted down to the boy's level, getting a kick out of the fact that the boy didn't recognize him out of his cowboy costume. "I'm Ian."

"I'm Casey." The boy put out his hand. "Please to meet you."

Ian grinned, solemnly shaking the hand that was offered to him, then rose to his feet. "I know some adults who could stand to learn a lesson in manners from you."

Casey beamed at the compliment.

She would have had to be blind not to notice the effect the man had on her family. Grudgingly, she gave him his due. "Well, you've won over my mother and my son in lightening speed."

His eyes met hers and, for a split second, she felt as if her mother and son had vanished and it was just the two of them. "Any chance of a trifecta?"

Rather than comment, Lisa thought it was safer just to retreat, at least for the time being. "I've got chicken parmesan on the stove." With that, she quickly turned away and went back to the kitchen.

Resting her hands of Casey's shoulders, Susan gave her daughter's guest an encouraging smile. "Lisa takes time."

"I've got nothing but," he replied. Craning his neck, glancing back toward where he assumed the kitchen was. He raised his voice. "Need any help in there?"

"No!" The answer came back so quickly, so emphatically, the single word sounded as if it were being shot out of a gun.

Casey tugged on his sweater again to gain his attention. "Do you like video games?"

Ian had no fear of admitting to any shortcomings. "You know, I've never really had a chance to play a video game."

To his surprise, the small boy nodded as if he expected the answer.

"Mom's not much good at it, either." He turned, looking up toward his grandmother. "But G-Mama is." He beamed at her and there was no mistaking the pride. "She can get all the bad guys really fast."

Ian laughed. That was probably due to the woman's firing range experience. "I bet she can."

Susan smiled at him. "I'm not the one you need to flatter."

"No flattery, just a feeling," Ian told her. "Besides, your daughter holds flattery suspect."

Susan's smile widened. She *really* liked this young man. "You're a pretty good judge of character, Mr.—?"

Formality didn't seem right here, especially since the woman was probably the same age his mother would have been, had his mother lived. "Ian," he supplied. "Just Ian."

Susan nodded. Ian it was. "So tell me, *just Ian,* what's a nice young man like you doing with a DUI on his record?"

So, Lisa had told her about that. "Being supremely stupid."

Susan looked pleased with his answer. "Just as long as you know."

When she finally stopped moving pots around,

straining spaghetti and drizzling mozzarella cheese over the string beans, Lisa could just about make out the soft murmur of voices coming from the other room. She'd half expected her mother or Ian or even Casey to show up in the kitchen after a few minutes, but she'd been left on her own, which ordinarily was the way she liked it.

Still, it made her curious. Just what was going on out there?

Under the pretext of bringing out the salad, she made her way from the kitchen to the small formal dining area. From there, she could see the living room.

Ian was sitting on the floor, tailor fashion, a game control in his hand. Her mother was standing over him, coaching, while Casey sat next to him, laughing as the action on the TV set continued nonstop.

Not exactly a Norman Rockwell setting, Lisa thought, but it came damn near close by today's standards.

Chapter Twelve

Ian found himself staying a good deal later than he had initially planned on. So late that Casey's official bedtime came and went, replaced by a second bedtime and then a third.

Finally, Lisa had no choice but to get tough with her son. He'd all but sealed himself to Ian's side, looking up at the man as if hero worship had always been a part of his makeup.

"I mean it, young man, you have *got* to go to bed."

Casey's eyes were drooping and only sheer stubborn will was holding them up. Any minute, he was going to have to use matchsticks to prop his eyelids open.

But he still refused to give in. "Just a little while longer, Mom," he pleaded with just a tad less verve than he'd had when he'd made his last two appeals. "Please?"

Lisa shook her head. Casey was going to be impossible to get up tomorrow morning. "No, not even for another second."

Casey shifted his eyes toward his newfound hero. "But I don't want to leave Ian," he cried.

This was where he said good night and went on his way, Ian thought. Then the boy wouldn't have a reason to resist. He didn't want to be the source of any friction between Lisa and her son.

But, like Casey, Ian realized, he was reluctant to call an end to the evening. "Tell you what, how about if I tell you a story?" he suddenly suggested. He raised his eyes to Lisa. "Provided of course that your mother doesn't mind."

"You mean read me a story," Casey corrected him politely.

Ian shook his head, smiling. Rising to his feet, he abandoned the video game controller he'd been working. "No, tell you one," he repeated.

Casey looked at him in awe. "You mean like make a story up?" he asked eagerly. "Right out of your head?"

It wasn't as spectacular a feat as Casey made it sound, Ian thought. He'd remembered a story he'd made up a long time ago. At the time it was to entertain Brenda. It now suddenly came back to him and he found himself wanting to share the story with this boy with the shining bright eyes and boundless energy.

So he nodded and echoed, "Right out of my head," and tried not to look as if he was laughing because he didn't want to hurt Casey's feelings.

"Okay." Shooting up to his feet, Casey grabbed his hand and began to pull him toward the stairs. "C'mon."

"Is it all right?" Ian asked Lisa.

"Of course it's all right," Susan told him since her daughter wasn't making any intelligible sounds in response to his question.

Being pulled away, Ian turned to look at Lisa over his shoulder. He liked the way amazement had taken possession of her face.

"We'll be upstairs," he told her, quickening his pace to keep up with Casey. They were at the top of the stairs before he even finished.

Susan rose from the sofa, turning so that her voice didn't carry up to the landing. She crossed her arms before her and gave her daughter a penetrating look. "Where's he been hiding all this time?"

Lisa shrugged. "Haven't a clue." She crossed her fingers that would be the end of it, but she knew she was being overly optimistic.

Her mother seemed to accept her answer. "You'd do well to give this one a chance."

Picking up one of the three controllers, Lisa

began to wrap the cord around the keypad to keep it from getting tangled with the others. "You make it sound like there's some kind of competition going on."

"Well, isn't there?" Susan asked. "A competition to see if any man can scale the bougainvillea-covered walls in order to gain access to the princess's heart?" She saw Lisa roll her eyes. "Like in those fairy tales you used to like to have me read to you."

That's exactly what they were, fairy tales. In real life, men didn't go out of their way to win anything but a beer-drinking contest. Matt hadn't been like that, but Matt was gone and he might have been the last of a what was a swiftly dying breed. "I'm not a little girl anymore, Mom."

"No," Susan said significantly, her eyes meeting her daughter's, "you're not." And then she crossed back to the closet, where Lisa had stashed her purse earlier. Opening the door, she took her jacket out.

As Lisa watched her mother put on the jacket, the panic that she had banished earlier, returned. Her mother was leaving. Leaving her with *him*. Her mouth suddenly felt dry.

"Where are you going?"

Susan slipped her purse onto her shoulder and tested the clasp to make sure it was closed. "I told Joe Majors that I'd be by for the poker game tonight."

Lisa glanced at the clock over the fireplace. It was after nine. "It's late."

Susan looked at her daughter, the look in her eyes saying, 'You're kidding, right?' "Not that late. Besides, I'm a big girl. I can stay up past nine."

She couldn't come right out and ask her to stay, couldn't tell her why she was afraid to be alone with Ian. So she searched for a way to make her point and yet not sound like such a coward about it.

"I meant—you're leaving me?"

Susan gave her a warm, encouraging smile. One that had sympathy written all over it. Lisa could feel herself rebelling—just as she figured her mother had to have known she would.

"You're a big girl, too," Susan was telling her, underscoring it with a quick pat on her cheek. "I won't be back until late. Unless, of course, Joe gets lucky." The wink was broad, sexy, its meaning clear.

She swore her mother had more energy than any five women her age. Hell, five women *her* age, Lisa thought. "Mother, you're fifty-one." She knew it would do no good to point out her mother's age, but she at least had to try.

Her mother turned the tables on her. "My point exactly. I'm not dead yet. And neither are you," she looked at her pointedly, "so stop acting that way and start living a little."

Lisa thought of all that she accomplished in a day and all that was left at the end of a day to still do. "If I lived any more, I'd have to be two people."

Susan paused to touch her face, caressing her

cheek. "You made a great dinner, Lisa. Now go have dessert."

Lisa opened her mouth and then closed it again. She didn't trust herself to reply, not right now.

She would have thought that her mother of all people would have understood how complicated all this was. Her parents had been married for a long time when a bullet had taken Alexander Kittridge from the wife and family who adored him. It seemed macabrely ironic that, married to a cop, the semipro football team coach would have walked in on a robbery that had gone bad.

From the footage that was obtained, it was obvious that the shooting was clearly a reflex action on the robber's part. But reflexive or intentional, her father was just as dead.

Her mother had gone through a prolonged period of mourning and then, one day, it was over. She shed the black veil that surrounded her heart and moved on. She got back into the game by going away with her father's best friend for a prolonged long weekend.

Well, maybe her mother could do that, she thought, heading for Casey's room, but she couldn't. She couldn't move on no matter what everyone else thought she could do. She just wasn't built like that.

Besides, even if she were, the possibility of pain at the end of any new venture into the choppy waters of romance was enough to deter her from ever entering the sailboat, much less piloting it out onto the sea.

Lisa heard the front door closing downstairs just as she came to the top of the landing.

Crossing the hallway, she softly approached Casey's bedroom. If he was falling asleep, the way she felt certain he *had* to be, she didn't want to make any noise and risk waking him up again. Casey was a wonderful kid, but he tended to get very grumpy when he didn't get enough sleep and he should have been asleep at least an hour ago.

The sound of Ian's voice, reciting something in a soft, easy cadence, drifted out of the room as she came closer. She stopped in the doorway, not wanting to come in, not wanting to intrude.

"And he stood there, at the top of the cliff, wondering if he should leap and find out if he did have those superpowers the unicorn had told him he had. The wind was very strong…" Ian's voice trailed off until he finally stopped. She saw the edge of a smile curving the corner of his mouth.

Finally, she asked, "So did he?"

Ian moved the comforter up higher, covering Casey better. He glanced at her over his shoulder. "Did he what?"

Wasn't he paying attention to himself? "Did he jump?"

Instead of giving her a yes or no answer, Ian

grinned. "Tune in tomorrow, same time, same place, to find out."

She crossed her arms before her, but there was amusement in her eyes. "Are you fishing for another invitation?"

Ian slipped out of the room. "Keep serving things like I had tonight and I'll be begging for another invitation."

She peered into the room, but there appeared to be nothing more for her to do. The boy was asleep, he was covered and peaceful. He hadn't even waited for her to come up to tell him good night, or to give him a good night kiss for that matter, she thought with just the minutest bit of sadness pricking her. But she understood. He was hungry for male companionship, male attention. Every boy needed some larger-than-life male figure in his life and although Frank came by and saw him pretty regularly, Frank was not his father and even though he was her brother, she had to admit that Frank was not dynamic.

She took a breath as she began to ease the door closed. "Thanks for getting him up to bed."

Ian took no credit. "He was set to collapse at any second." He nodded toward the inside of the room just before she shut the door. "Aren't you going to close the light?"

Lisa surprised him by shaking her head. "He's afraid of the dark."

Lots of kids were, Ian thought. He had been. His

grandfather had ridiculed him and insisted on keeping the light off. The two times he'd disobeyed and switched the light back on again, he'd gotten a beating. So he'd spent terrified nights in the dark until he'd finally realized that the monsters were not in the closet or under his bed, they were out and about in the world.

He looked at her with interest. "And you're not insisting that he get over it?"

Lisa led the way back downstairs. She couldn't quite make out what he was thinking, if he thought that she was being too soft or if he thought she was being kind. But, either way, it wouldn't change anything. She let her heart guide her when it came to raising Casey.

"He will, in time." She didn't add that she spoke from experience, that at Casey's age she was terrified of the dark and could only sleep if there was enough light in her bedroom to power Las Vegas. Her mother never said anything, she just left the light on. And, eventually, her fears faded and she learned to like the dark.

Ian nodded his approval. "Person after my own heart." At the bottom of the stairs, he looked around. "Speaking of mothers, where's yours?"

"Out playing poker." She tried to sound as if it didn't matter to her one way or another, that her mother's absence didn't suddenly make her feel this side of vulnerable. "She said to tell you good night."

"Poker?" He grinned as he asked, tickled by the image of Susan Kittridge sitting at a table, surrounded by gruff men and an impenetrable wreath of smoke, boldly bluffing her way from hand to hand.

"My dad taught her to play. She's almost addicted to it. Luckily, she doesn't believe in betting big." Her mother had gotten that under control a long time ago. Now she and her friends played for points. Big winners came away with ten, fifteen dollars after a full night of playing.

Nerves were beginning to play leapfrog with one another inside of her. Pretty soon, she wouldn't be able to take in a deep breath.

"So," she said a little too cheerfully, "I guess you'll be going."

He grinned, making no move to head for the front door. "Is that a suggestion, Kitty, or a not-too-subtle request?"

A plea was more like it, she thought. The longer that he stayed, the less resistance she seemed to have toward him. "I just thought that it was getting later and…"

"And tomorrow's a school night," he finished, his eyes teasing her.

He made it sound like a joke, but both she and Casey had to be up early. There was a Thanksgiving party at school and she still hadn't really gone shopping for herself and her family.

"Something like that."

He knew he should bow out gracefully now, especially since she had all but asked him to go. But he found that he still really didn't want to. Not just yet.

So he bargained with himself and remained for a few minutes longer, swearing silently that he'd be out the door soon, very soon.

In the meantime, he needed to be honest with her. "This is going to go further, you know."

Oh God, they were going to talk about the elephant in the living room, acknowledging him and giving him a life of his own. She tried to be flippant. "Are you warning me or making a prophesy?"

"Maybe both."

His eyes were melting her resolve, not to mention her knees. She wished she were sitting down.

"And why would you be warning me?" she wanted to know. Most men attempted to stealthily move in, they didn't issue alerts.

Very lightly, he skimmed his fingers along the outline of her hair. He saw her struggle not to shiver in response. He felt the same sort of electricity shimmy up his spine.

"Because I think you're as nervous as I am about it."

"Nervous?" she echoed. "Why would you be nervous? I thought this was what men did—" When he continued looking at her, waiting for her to continue, she added, "—have conquests."

He knew she didn't believe that. At least not about him. Not in this particular situation. "I think we both know this is something more than that."

Oh God, she could barely breathe. The air had solidified into chunks of ice, embedding itself in her lungs. She could almost feel it. "And what is it?" she managed to ask.

He didn't answer immediately. Instead, he smiled at her. "Do you moonlight for the CIA?"

She ran her tongue along her bottom lip to keep it from sealing itself to her upper one. "Don't change the subject."

He felt himself growing aroused, just watching the tip of her tongue move along. Wanting to mimic its path. "That's just it, I'm not sure what the subject is. Or what *this* is, just that I've never been in this place before."

"This place?" she repeated, wanting to be absolutely sure she understood as much as she could. Because right at this moment, she felt hopelessly lost, without a single bread crumb to show her the way out.

"Emotionally," he clarified.

And just what kind of load of goods was he trying to sell her? "You've never been with a woman before."

He heard her mocking tone. She'd misunderstood. "Oh, I've been with a woman before, with a lot of women."

If he thought he was going to impress her by

bragging, then she'd completely misjudged him. She wanted him out of here. *Now.* "I see."

If her voice was any icier, he was going to need a fur coat. "Physically," he emphasized.

Lisa stared at him. "And you're telling me that this is more."

His eyes were holding her prisoner. "I'm telling you this is more."

Why did she believe him, she demanded silently. "You're making it very hard to keep you at arm's length."

He took her by the wrists and, with one on either side of him, drew her closer. So close that she was inside an embrace without his having to enfold his arms around her.

"Then don't."

The heat from his body transferred itself to her, calling to every fiber of her being. Burning down the last of her defenses.

And then he was kissing her, slanting his mouth over hers, first gently, then with more and more force, more and more passion. She pulled her wrists free. But it wasn't to push him away, it was to thread her arms around his neck.

When she finally came up for air, she made one last weak stab at saving herself. Because it had come down to that. She was going under quickly and she knew it.

"Ian—"

"Shh," he murmured, his breath feathering along her face. He brought his lips down to hers again, feeling everything inside of him ignite as he kissed her one more time.

The last time, he promised himself.

But it wasn't the last time. Because he kissed her over and over again, his mouth taking hers as the urgency within him built to incredible proportions.

He knew the signs.

If he didn't stop now, there would be no stopping and she had been reluctant. It wasn't fair to overwhelm her this way. He could feel her compliance as her body stretched against his, even now silently surrendering.

He wanted her to do it by choice, not because he'd seduced her.

With monumental effort and a reluctance that was completely unfamiliar to him, Ian drew his head back. "I guess I'd better hit the road."

"You do," she told him, trying very hard not to gasp for air, "and I might have to hurt you."

He was unprepared for the amount of strength and warmth that flooded him. "Is that your subtle way of saying you want me to stay?"

She'd risen up on her toes, her body fitting against his even more tightly. "That's my only way of saying I want you to stay."

The grin was sensual as it took possession of his lips. And of her.

"No," he breathed, curling his fingers along her temple, moving the hair away from her face, his body aware of every inch of hers, "not your only way. Not by a long shot."

It was out of his hands. Out of hers. The bonfire no longer could be controlled. There was only one way to extinguish it.

And they both knew it.

"I'm staying the night, Kitty," he whispered against her lips.

She knew that. But to hear him say it caused all sorts of things to go off inside of her, like a belated Mardi Gras celebration. Every single pulse point in her body went into overdrive as she took his hand in hers and silently led him up the stairs.

To her bedroom.

Her brain in a swirling haze, she was surprised that she remembered the way. And that her knees didn't give out beneath her before she reached it.

Chapter Thirteen

Click.

The sound of her bedroom door slipping into its frame as the lock simultaneously found its mate, seemed to vibrate through Lisa's body.

Or was she just trembling inwardly from anticipation?

She wasn't sure.

All she knew was that this was finally happening between them, they were finally coming together. Despite all the safeguards she'd put into place, despite all the excuses she'd hand-fed herself about why this *shouldn't* be happening, it was and she was glad, oh so very glad.

Everything inside of her was scrambling, battening down the hatches and bracing itself for one hell of a hurricane.

It had been so long, so terribly long, since she had been with a man, since her body had felt itself tottering on the edge of an eruption.

Eagerness seized her. Lisa swiftly pulled the jacket from Ian's shoulders, tugging it down his arms. Attacking the shirt that was beneath.

All the while, her lips were sealed to his and she felt the curve of his mouth against hers.

Probably laughing at her, she thought.

If she were in her right mind, if her body wasn't humming like a freshly struck, primed tuning fork, she would have pulled away the moment she'd felt his lips curving. She would have said something about this being a mistake and cloaked herself in whatever dignity she had left as she sent him on his way.

It was still a mistake, but she had no cloak, no desire to slip one over her shoulders, no desire to end this. She had left her right mind the moment she had first kissed him.

The desire that beat so swiftly, so erratically in her chest was completely centered on Ian and on this moment.

"Are you sure?"

His question came to her wrapped in a cloud. "I'm sure, I'm sure," she swore. If he were to stop now, she'd probably go up in flames on her own.

A moan escaped her lips before she could stop it as she felt his hands on her, felt him drawing her pullover up over her head, felt his hands covering her breasts even as they were still contained in the bra she'd put on at the last moment. A bra that was impossibly slight, sheer and provocatively sexy. It was definitely not the kind of bra she'd wear to a PTA meeting, even underneath two layers of clothing.

Lisa felt the bra's clasp loosen at her back, felt the material slipping a fraction at a time from her skin until finally the straps pooled along her elbows and then her forearms, exposing her to his hot gaze.

The next moment she moaned again, dropping her head back as Ian's lips moved from her mouth, down along her throat, to the expanse of skin beneath.

She caught her lip between her teeth as she felt the tip of his tongue encircle first one nipple, then move to the other.

Hot shards of desire shot through her upper torso, and fed into her very core.

Coming to, Lisa frantically went to work on the rest of his clothing, trying to divest him from it as quickly as humanly possible.

She thought she heard a low, throaty laugh and ignored it. She didn't want to think, to analyze, she just wanted for once in her well-ordered, overly scheduled life, to *feel*.

Damn but she got his blood racing, Ian thought.

He'd felt himself hardening, wanting her from

the moment her perfume had wafted to him, taking him prisoner. It had been a struggle to appear unaffected all through dinner, all through the conversation afterward. He'd fought not to think of her, but it was hopeless. Even as he sat, telling Casey the story that had ultimately put him to sleep, all he could think of was making love with her.

Because once he made love with her, then maybe this madness—because no sane man could possibly feel like this—would finally stop. Maybe then he finally could get back to his life and try to get it back on its solitary, isolated track.

But if that was the plan, to make love, get cured, and then go, somehow, he lost his way the moment he was alone with her. All the control he'd always been so proud of was nowhere in sight. He just wanted to please her, to possess her and to find in the morning that it all hadn't been a dream.

Ian discovered that the terrain in this brand-new world he found himself in was like quicksand. The further out he ventured, the less sure his footing was, the deeper he sank.

And he didn't care.

At least, not now. Later, later he'd care, later he would try to mend fences and get himself back to where he wanted to be. Later he'd be horrified at just how badly he'd lost control. But right now, the only place he wanted to be was with her. Making love to her, making love *with* her.

Every time she reacted to him, the sound of her quick intake of breath, her barely suppressed moan, made him feel as if he were ten feet tall and bullet-proof.

He liked the fact that Lisa was reacting to *him*. It was raw. It was pure.

He had her naked and they had tumbled back onto the bed. Holding her hands out so that they were spread far on either side of her, Ian proceeded to anoint her whole body with his lips, with his teeth and with his tongue, managing to reduce her to a squirming, panting mass of femininity.

Doing it until he felt that he could no longer hold himself in check. The scent of her filled his head, urging him on. He didn't like this, didn't like that he couldn't just separate himself and observe from a distance. Didn't like that he was immersing himself completely in her.

But he was and he couldn't stop it.

And then he came for her. Came to her. Filling her and himself at the same moment.

The moment she felt him begin, she lifted her hips as far as she could, drawing him into her. She reveled in the way the rhythm came for them, over-taking them and continuing to build as his hips moved in time with hers. Faster, faster until the rush came, washing over both of them.

She sealed her mouth to his to keep from scream-ing out his name. As it was, she felt it echoing into his mouth just as the rapture came for her, leaving in its place a mindless, sweaty creature who didn't know where he ended and she began.

He left her breathless. So breathless that she could hardly draw any air in.

She felt Ian's weight as the euphoria faded into the mists. His arms tightened around her rather than loosened. And then she felt him shifting so that he was above her again.

The first thing she saw was his smile. It was wide and it warmed her because it spread not only to his lips but to his eyes as well.

"Wow."

Lisa smiled in response to the sentiment. "You're a man of few words."

Ian thought of the blank screen that mocked him every morning, haunted him every night. "You don't know the half of it."

That wasn't just a flippant answer, she thought. Something was going on, something beneath the surface. She found herself wanting to know. Caring. "Then tell me."

No, he wasn't going to ruin this with any kind of confessions. Besides, talking about the writer's block that had eaten its way into the fabric of his brain was somehow too personal. Even far more personal than what had just happened here between them.

So he shook his head, shifting again, this time

laying down beside her. "Maybe some other time," he said carelessly.

She felt empty the second he drew away.

But then he was next to her, his arms around her as he pulled her to him. Holding her in the shelter formed by his body.

This was way too intimate, she thought. Vainly she tried to reconstruct events, wondering how she'd gotten to this place.

She turned her head so that their faces were less than two inches apart. As if they were always meant to be together.

But that, of course, was a lie. "Did you know?" she asked.

He toyed with a strand of her hair, pushing it away from her face. Wanting her all over again. "Did I know what?"

She took a breath. Her breasts moved against him, sending renewed shafts of excitement through her that she struggled to keep in check. "That the evening was going to go like this?"

"No, I didn't know." That was the truth. He hadn't known for certain. "But I hoped," he added in a low, confidential voice.

He was leaning his cheek against the top of her head and she could feel his every word, could feel his breath along her scalp and could almost feel the smile she just knew was on his face.

She didn't want this to end, but it had to. She still

needed to get up early in the morning and there was the matter of her mother coming back again tonight. Although Susan Kittridge had already given her her blessings and all but shoved her into Ian's arms, she would rather not have her mother catch her entertaining someone in her bed.

"Well, I'd better get dressed," she began haltingly, an awkwardness suddenly descending on her.

What was it that you said to someone after the fact? She and Matt had known one another for a long time so the conversation between them after lovemaking had always been easy.

But she was still feeling her way around this man and now that the passion had subsided to a manageable, throbbing, palpitating mass, she was left feeling as if she were all elbows and knees.

"Why?" He caught her wrist, holding it lightly but still preventing her from leaving her bed. "Do you sleep with your clothes on?"

She wished she had a few clothes on her now, or at least within easy reach. "No."

"Well, then why do you want to get dressed?" Still holding one wrist prisoner, he rolled over so that he was propped up on his elbow, looking down at her. He tugged the corner of the sheet up so that she could cover herself if she wanted to. To keep from embarrassing her, he looked only into her eyes.

She could feel her heart begin to race again. "Because I can't just lay here, naked—"

"Works for me," he quipped. "But if you're determined not to just lie here before you fall asleep, I've got something for you to do."

The next moment, he was bringing his mouth down to hers again.

Oh, hell, in for a penny, in for a pound, Lisa thought, surrendering to the overwhelming desire that had begun to build up again within her.

She threaded her arms around his neck and met him half way.

She hadn't expected him to be here, not after Tuesday night. Tuesday night that burned its way into early Wednesday morning.

And she had reminded Ian about his volunteering to serve turkey on Thursday when they had finally parted and he'd gotten into his car. Dan had been seated, sleepy-eyed in the driver's seat, waiting to take him home, and Ian had nodded, telling her he remembered.

But she hadn't really expected him to show up at the shelter today. Certainly not early enough to be put to work by Raul. People like Ian Malone always made promises, sometimes even well-intentioned promises, that they never kept. Never even remembered.

But he had and he was here. One of the first people to arrive. He even beat her by twenty minutes.

Even more overwhelming was that he could cook.

That *really* surprised her. She hadn't thought he could do that outside of the bedroom.

Dear God, more than twenty-four hours later and her body still felt as if it were tingling. She'd never had anyone make love to her so completely before. Not even Matt. Ian had managed to pull climax after climax out of her, playing her as if she were some finely tuned instrument.

Which only told her how much he got around. And she didn't need a player.

She told herself that over and over again, all day Wednesday, all this morning when she'd gotten up at the crack of dawn to first prepare the turkey that she was serving to her family.

She didn't want a player.

Too bad she couldn't seem to convince herself, no matter how much she argued. But that could have something to do with the fact that every fiber of her being was moist with wanting.

Wouldn't be in this state if you just went out once in a while, she thought as she stirred some of the cranberry sauce to keep a skin from forming on it, *like a normal, red-blooded woman.*

But she wasn't the type. Wasn't the type to be with anyone she didn't want to turn into a permanent person in her life.

Until now, she silently insisted. This man was not permanent and what had happened between them was just one of those insane things that happen when chemistry is brought into play.

The second she saw him, walking into the common room from the kitchen, an apron tied tightly around his trim waist, holding a long, rectangular silver pan of steaming mashed potatoes in his hands, Lisa knew she was in trouble.

Her heart had done a backward flip and her stomach had tightened so hard she thought her spleen was going to run for cover.

She was twenty-nine years old for God sakes. Much too old to be experiencing this schoolgirl crush that seemed to be hemming her in.

She did her best to sound very businesslike as he made his way to her end of the steam table. "What are you doing here?"

He smiled at her, a little bemused. "You're way too young for Alzheimer's, aren't you, Kitty?" he teased her, setting the pan down. "You told me to be here, remember?" He leaned into her so that his words wouldn't be overheard by anyone else. "Just before you singed off all my clothes."

She cleared her throat, hoping that the lighting in the common room wasn't good enough to highlight what she knew had to be red splotches racing up her cheeks. "I know what I told you, but I expected you to be spending the holidays with someone."

"I am," he told her glibly.

"Who?" *None of your damn business, that's who,* she sternly lectured herself.

He was still leaning over her, but this time, his voice softened ever so slightly.

"You," he replied. "And I'm spending it here."

This was far too sad a place to remain for the whole day. Those that had somewhere to go, did. "And no place else?"

He didn't answer. Instead, he focused on the reason he was there. He indicated the rectangular pan he was still holding. "This is getting heavy."

She doubted it. He had muscles that would make all but the most dedicated bodybuilder envious. But holding the pan was uncomfortable and awkward, she'd give him that.

"Put it there," she pointed toward the large rectangular slot beside the slicked turkey on the steam table. He angled it in. The clatter of metal against metal was heard.

When Muriel brought out the mixed vegetables, they were all ready.

The older woman nodded toward one of the teenaged volunteers, a tall, blond-haired boy who looked as if he weighed all of a hundred and thirty pounds by choice. He was at the door that separated the common room from the living quarters where all the people at the shelter and the homeless who had come off the street were gathered, waiting. Waiting to take part in a celebration that linked them to everyone else in the country.

"Open the doors, Jerry," Muriel instructed in her cheery, high-pitched voice, every syllable enunciated crisply like a general sounding a charge.

The second Jerry opened the doors, he stepped to the side to get out of the way.

Residents and the people off the streets began filing in, maintaining a surprising amount of order. Some came neatly dressed or at least washed, others were disheveled even though they had done their best to appear presentable.

But they all came hungry.

They had to have fed more than five hundred strong, Lisa thought. Muriel had told her that there had been a larger than usual amount of donated turkeys. She had a feeling she knew where the extra supply had come from.

When she turned to Muriel and asked, she was told that the card had simply born the word "anonymous" on it.

That would be his style, Lisa thought, slanting a glance to her left where Ian was standing, serving what was quickly getting to be the last of the mashed potatoes.

Ian was a hard man to read, she thought. A hard man, but a good one. A man, she felt deep down, who needed saving. Needed something to live for. They weren't all that different, he and she.

She drew her courage to her, knowing that if she didn't get this out quickly, she wouldn't get it out at all. And that would be a shame.

"Would you like to come over and have Thanksgiving dinner with my family?"

Ian turned to look at her, his expression telling her that he was certain he'd imagined it. Dark eyebrows drew together in concentration. The person on the other side of the table stood patiently waiting for his mashed potatoes.

"You're inviting me?"

Lisa nodded toward the person who held his tray out before him. Ian swiftly gave the man his potatoes. At this point, he was on automatic pilot.

"I don't like to think of someone with nowhere to go on the holidays," she told him honestly.

"So the invitation is just a natural extension of your charity?"

She couldn't read his expression. Had she insulted him? Hurt his feelings? She hadn't meant to. Things had been a lot simpler when she'd thought of him as a self-centered, overly indulgent jerk.

"Don't analyze it," she hissed under her breath. "Do you or don't you want to come over?"

It was on the tip of his tongue to turn her down, just as he had turned down Marcus two days ago and just as he had turned down Dan who had surprised him this morning by asking him if he would like to join his wife and his boys for dinner. After all, it was his cardinal rule that if he couldn't be away for the holidays, which this year he obviously couldn't, then he still didn't have to share them with anyone. That way, he could pretend the holidays didn't exist. And if they didn't exist, then it didn't hurt to be without his family on the special days.

But it was hard to pretend the holidays didn't exist when he was standing here, feeding the masses. He might as well go all the way, he thought.

"Okay. I'd like that, Kitty."

He caught the smile on her lips just as she turned her head away. Something about the sight of it helped keep his dread of the holidays at bay.

Chapter Fourteen

The voices were back.

Ian's eyes flew open, jolted out of a deep sleep.

He still heard them.

They'd begun softly, in his dreams, and continued now that he was actually awake. It'd been so long since he'd heard them that he had begun to think he'd imagined the phenomena in the first place. Until they reappeared.

They were the voices of his characters. The ones he pinned down on paper and then brought into existence. Characters so vivid they were just waiting for him to open the gates and give them life and breath.

The voices that had initially made him a writer.

Anticipation telegraphed itself through Ian and he jumped out of bed. He hadn't felt this excited about his craft in a long time. Without bothering to brush his teeth or to do any of the things that civilized people did every morning when they left the shelter of their beds, preparing to meet another day head on, he simply ran down to his study and sat down in front of the computer.

The moment he planted his seat on the chair, he half expected the voices to vanish, to realize that he'd only been dreaming about the way things had once been, when writing had been his salvation.

But the voices didn't vanish and this wasn't a dream or even wishful thinking on his part. What he was being privy to in the recesses of his head was a scene. A scene from the book he was supposed to be writing. The book he hadn't been writing for all these months. Granted the scene was out of order, but it didn't matter.

What mattered was that the words were there. The characters were there. Taking shape right before his mind's eye.

Ian couldn't type fast enough to keep up. He had to keep stopping to fill in the words he'd whizzed by the first time.

When he finished, when the burst of energy subsided and the voices finally retreated back into the mists from whence they came, to his amazement, Ian discovered that he'd written a good chapter and a half.

A chapter and a half after *nothing* for nine months.

It didn't matter that he'd plucked it out of the last third, didn't matter that he still had to polish the chapter to get it to stand up on its own and that he needed to write a hell of a lot of other chapters in front of it before these pages could slip into their rightful place. None of that mattered. What mattered was that he'd written.

He'd written.

After a drought of more than nine months, words had suddenly come flooding back to him so fast, so furiously that he could barely navigate the waters.

Wow.

The single word throbbed and echoed within Ian's brain. It was the same word he'd used the first time that he had made love with Kitty. The first time but not the only time, he thought, a fond smile curving his mouth. They'd gotten together several more times since that first night. Made love several more times. Starting with the very next Thursday.

He'd shared Thanksgiving dinner with her and her family, then waited out her son and her mother until both had gone off to bed and her brother Frank and his girlfriend had gone home. He'd had to tell Casey another story he made up, but it didn't matter. The prize at the end of the road made it all worth it.

He had remained with her as long as he could, with the promise of dawn tiptoeing on the doorsill before he'd called for a taxi. It was much too late in his opinion—or too early depending on the point of view—to rouse Dan to come get him.

There'd been a few more evenings since then, evenings that were gradually transforming him, making him feel as if he were someone else. Making him feel as if he'd been reborn. And that was due to the fact that he was growing attached to Kitty.

Hell, he wasn't growing attached, he *was* attached, so much so that it worried him. It brought back memories. And it made him uneasy about what might be waiting to overtake him just around the bend. But not uneasy enough to break it off. Even if it was the right thing to do, the safe thing to do, he couldn't step back into the shadows again. Not after being with her.

The very thought created a warmth within him.

Was that it? Was making love with Kitty, looking forward to seeing her, to seeing her son and even her mother, looking forward to being part of a family unit after so many years in emotional exile, was that the reason the dark, oppressive curtain had finally lifted from around his brain? Was the relief, the contentment he felt around the woman, around her family, allowing the voices to return? Allowing him to be what he was meant to be. A writer.

The voices.

He laughed softly to himself. He knew it sounded strange and he didn't mention it to anyone for that reason. If he did, whoever he told would probably think he was on his way to becoming a deranged serial killer. Weren't they the ones who heard voices in their heads? But in his case, it was different.

Done for now, Ian leaned back in his chair, lacing his hands behind his head. He stared at the screen, reading the words for the first time. After a bit, he hit the combination of keys that saved his work for him.

An incredible peacefulness descended over him.

He was writing again. Hot damn, he was writing again!

Uttering a whoop of triumph, he spun himself around on the swivel chair, completing three circles before he finally stopped. If Kitty were here, he would have thrown his arms around her and hugged her to him for all he was worth.

Something to look forward to, he promised himself as he got up. After he got her alone tonight.

But first, he thought, heading out of the room and toward the stairs, he needed a shower.

Passing the phone in his bedroom, he stopped impulsively and picked up the receiver. He hit the keypad, tapping out the numbers that would connect him to her cell phone. After three rings, he heard a pick up on the other end of the line.

"Hi, Kitty, I—"

"This is Lisa's phone. Lisa's busy right now, but as soon as she has a free moment, she'll call back. Provided you leave your name and number at the sound of the beep. Go for it."

He laughed. Even the message on the cell phone was typical Kitty. "Hi, Kitty. It's me. I just wanted to hear the sound of your voice. Looking forward to seeing you tonight. I have something to tell you."

There, that sounded mysterious enough, he thought, hanging up. Tonight, he was going to tell her what he did for a living. And how she was responsible for getting him back to it.

Whistling, he walked into the shower.

Lisa moved around the kitchen, humming. She'd woken up to find a message on her cell phone from Ian. The man got up with the birds, she thought. So much for thinking he liked to sleep in.

Learned something new every day. Her grin widened.

She paused to get herself a cup of coffee. What was he going to tell her, she wondered. Lisa could hardly stop smiling long enough to take a sip of the dark, bitter brew.

Okay, she was happy. She held the cup in both hands. So happy, she was scared. Scared that it was all going to blow up in her face, just the way it had last time, when Matt died. Scared that she was going to invest her heart in someone and then have the life crushed out of it for some reason.

But it was too late to worry about what-ifs. She wasn't going to invest her heart in him. She already had. There was no kidding herself. Little by little, bit by bit, that charming man with the gorgeous eyes and killer smile had wormed his way into the burnt ashes of her heart and made it flourish again.

She could only hope that she had done the same with him.

But if she hadn't why would he have said yes? she reasoned, taking another long sip. She'd invited him to spend the Christmas holidays with her. With them, she corrected silently. Her, Casey and her mother. They always went up to Big Bear Lake for Christmas. A friend of her mother's from the force, Kyle Buchanan, had a cabin up there, he let them stay in while he and his wife went to Florida for the holidays every year. Kyle always told them that they were doing him a favor, house-sitting during the holidays.

Lisa smiled to herself. It gave Casey an opportunity to have a white Christmas. And this year, she was going to have an opportunity to have what she hadn't had for years now. Someone special to love for Christmas.

She tightened her hands around the mug, thinking about being stretched out before a warm fire with Ian.

Winter break officially began today. No more

school for two weeks. She'd woken up making lists in her head of things she needed to bring with her to the cabin. This year, she wanted it to be special.

This year, it *was* special, she amended.

God but all this happiness did scare her.

"Well, you certainly look pleased with yourself."

Lisa turned around on the stool to see her mother making her way into the kitchen, her eyes still partially shut as she smelled her way to a very much needed first cup of coffee.

She pushed a mug toward her mother. Susan scooped it up without missing a beat as she picked up the coffee pot from the burner with the other. The scent of rich coffee drifted through the air as liquid met mug.

"I am." Lisa paused for a moment, wondering how to word this. She decided to just say it without any preamble. "Mom, I'm bringing a guest to the cabin this year."

"Oh?" Taking her mug of pitch-black coffee liquid in her hand, Susan sat down beside her daughter and waited. "Who?" she finally asked, trying to sound curious.

For a former policewoman, her mother was a terrible actress, Lisa thought. "I think you can guess."

But Susan shook her head. She wanted confirmation. "I never gamble away from the poker table."

Lisa'd never understood that, but she was relieved nonetheless. "Ian."

"Yes!" Susan cried, surprising Lisa as she fisted her hand and jerked it down in a quick motion signifying victory. And then she gave Lisa a long, penetrating look. "About time."

Yes, she supposed maybe it was. And maybe she'd held back so that she'd be ready when he came along. There was no way of knowing.

"Maybe." Finishing her coffee, she placed the cup on the counter and slid off the stool. "Look, I'm going to need a lot of things from the supermarket today before we leave. Do you think you could go shopping for me?"

Susan nodded. She took another long, fortifying sip. "No problem." Her curiosity got the better of her. "But you don't have to go to school anymore," she reminded her daughter. "What are you going to be doing?"

For a second, she thought about being mysterious, but she was too happy to pull it off. Lisa grinned again as she headed out of the kitchen and toward the stairs. "Just a little last-minute Christmas shopping."

Susan leaned back against the stool and called after her, "I still take a size ten."

"Not for you," Lisa sang back.

Susan hadn't thought it would be, but she pretended to frown for form's sake. "Rats." She hid a wide smile behind her coffee mug.

About time, she thought again.

* * *

When she got to the mall, it occurred to Lisa that she had absolutely no idea what to get Ian. She'd always prided herself on giving gifts that meant something, not grabbing the first thing she came to but matching the gift to the person she was giving them to. But when it came to Ian, she realized that she had no idea what kind of music he liked or what kind of movies he watched or the sort of television programs he enjoyed.

She didn't know if he was like most men and into gadgets, either digital or analog. He'd never even mentioned sports so, for all she knew, he didn't care for any of the games that played such a great part in so many men's lives.

He probably didn't even golf, she thought darkly as she passed a sporting-goods store.

Then she noticed a bookstore right beside the sporting-goods store. One of those chains that had made its way across the country. She stopped to look in the window.

Ian liked books, she thought suddenly. He had to because she'd heard him reading to the children at the shelter as well as spinning all those original stories for Casey.

Casey. It had gotten to the point that her son absolutely refused to go to bed unless Ian told him a story. And there was always a new one. She didn't know how Ian did it. When she'd asked him where he got all those stories from, Ian had shrugged modestly and told her that he read a lot and just seemed to retain things. When he told Casey a story, he'd just mix things up, taking a little from here, a little from there and creating something new.

That was when she'd asked Ian what kind of stories he liked best. He'd answered without hesitation that he enjoyed science fiction, always had. He'd had a funny expression on his face when he said it and she just assumed it had triggered a memory for him. She'd left it alone, not wanting to drudge up anything that might be painful for him to recall.

Okay, science fiction, she thought. That was a good start. Too bad she hadn't had her wits about her and asked which authors he liked. But at the time, she hadn't thought she'd be buying him a gift.

Now there was nothing else she wanted more than to buy him the perfect gift.

Lisa made her way through the store, vying for space amid the rest of the holiday shoppers, searching for the science-fiction section. She'd always loved books, but even so, she knew absolutely nothing about science fiction. It didn't interest her. She tended toward biographies and books that dealt with history, both real and fictionalized. However, mysteries had always been her favorite reading material.

She wondered if she could get Ian a book that was a mixture of science fiction and mystery. That way, when he was finished with it, she could read it, too, and then they could talk about it.

Or was that being too optimistic? Did men talk about books?

You're getting ahead of yourself. First find him a book, she told herself.

Lisa was running out of time and she still hadn't found the right section. Looking around, she spotted a rather harried-looking salesclerk and made her way over to the young woman. "Where can I find the science-fiction section?"

Rather than answer, the clerk pointed. The next second, she was being buttonholed by another customer. She was on her own, Lisa thought, working her way over to where the clerk pointed.

The science-fiction section took over two complete bookcases going from floor to ceiling. Current bestsellers were displayed by new hardbacks, followed by classic bestsellers and then, finally, rows and rows of paperbacks, all arranged in alphabetical order by author.

God, but there were a lot to choose from, she thought, momentarily overwhelmed.

She discovered that the classic bestsellers also contained reduced hardback copies, often at less than half price because the books had all gone into paperback editions.

Reduced meant she could buy two instead of

one, she reasoned. Two gifts were always better than just one.

She continued to pick and choose. Because she was unfamiliar with any of the authors, she let herself be drawn by first the cover, then the back copy. Methodically working her way across, Lisa had read the back copies of twelve books before she came to it.

The last book that B. D. Brendan had written. *Ghosts Among Us.*

Thinking that this might be something that Ian would enjoy since there were so many accolades for the author embossed on the front cover, Lisa took the book off the shelf and flipped open to the first page.

After she read it, she turned to the next page. And the next. The style was easygoing, entertaining and, she thought chewing on her lower lip, vaguely familiar. But that didn't really seem possible. She'd never read a science-fiction book in her life and she was probably one of the few people living on the planet who had never even seen *one* of the *Star Wars* movies.

But it still felt familiar somehow.

It wasn't until she flipped over the book and looked at the back copy that her breath literally stopped in her throat.

There was a brief biography of the book's author along with a photograph. The photo was black and white, but it might as well have been in vivid color. It jumped right out at her.

She knew that face. Knew it almost as well as she knew her own.

A mass of colors were suddenly swirling through her head and everything around her felt as if it had slipped into another dimension, moving about her in slow motion.

There had to be some mistake. An error had been made at the printer's, although where the printer would have gotten a photograph of Ian Malone, she hadn't the slightest idea.

Holding the book, she made her way past the new arrivals and the classic section to look at the collection of paperbacks. It took her a few seconds to find B. D. Brendan's area on the shelf.

He'd written a lot of books, she discovered. Taking out the first, she flipped it over only to find a description of the book, no photograph. The same was true of the second and the third. She went through every different title.

Brendan's photograph was on only three different books. Three photographs, taken at different times. He had on different clothes, wore a slightly different hairstyle. There were three different expressions: serious, semi-serious, smiling.

They were all of Ian.

Her heart felt like lead within her chest.

She held onto the book with icy fingers. Her head began to hurt.

This wasn't a mistake. Ian Malone wasn't Ian at

all. He was someone named B. D. Brendan. From the looks of it, this Brendan was apparently a writer of some fame.

And she hadn't known. Hadn't even had so much as a single clue.

God, but he must have thought she was an idiot. She was a teacher, she should have known who he was if he was famous in his field. Should she have? Had he been laughing at her from the start?

Numb, still clutching the first book she'd taken from the shelf, she made her way up to the front counter. A new register opened just as she reached it.

The woman beckoned her over and smiled when she saw her selection. "It's an excellent book," she enthused. "The critics were a little hard on him, but what do they know? Everyone I know who read it loved it. I read it twice myself. You have to read these things at least twice to get the full impact of them. I can't wait for his new one to come out."

"His new one?" The words dribbled from her lips in slow motion.

The clerk nodded. "They just keep getting better and better, but it seems like it's been forever since this one came out." The clerk rang up the sale, then looked at the photograph on the back. Her eyes sparkled as she looked at her. "He's a real hunk, don't you think?"

"A hunk," Lisa echoed. What had he thought of her? When she'd asked him if he'd ever thought about writing, how had he kept from laughing out loud at her?

And why hadn't he told her who he was? Did he think she'd want something from him if she knew that he was this famous writer? That she'd treat him differently? Did he trust her that little?

Did he trust her at all?

And why should she trust him, Lisa demanded silently. He had kept his very identity a secret from her. What was she doing, sleeping with a man she didn't know?

"Enjoy your book," the clerk said cheerfully as she handed her the bag with her purchase.

Lisa was too upset to say anything in response as she hurried out of the bookstore.

Chapter Fifteen

"Looks like she's waiting for you."

Ian could hear the grin in Dan's voice as he pulled the car up into Providence Shelter's parking lot later that day. The "she" Dan was referring to was Lisa.

At first, Ian smiled to himself and then he took a closer look at her expression as she approached his car. It was far from friendly.

"More like she's gunning for me," Ian commented. He hadn't a clue as to what would cause her to be so angry. Had the boiler blown up?

The second he opened the door to get out, Lisa was on him. She pushed the door shut so hard with the flat of her hand, it seemed to vibrate.

"Who the hell are you?" she demanded hotly.

Confused, he stared at her. "You know who I am."

"Apparently not."

To underscore her statement, she shoved the book into his midsection so hard, it momentarily sent all the air out of him. An incredible pain came rushing in. His disorientation vanished as he looked down at the book he'd grabbed before it fell to the unevenly paved ground.

Ghosts Among Us. His last book.

She knew who he was. And he hadn't been the one to tell her.

The thought telegraphed itself through his mind, along with a shaft of uneasiness. He should have never kept it from her for so long.

"I can explain," he began.

"Save it," Lisa snapped, her eyes narrowing. "I don't want to hear it."

When he reached for her, she pulled away. As if she'd rather be touched by a rattlesnake than him. "Kitty, be reasonable."

Her eyes were flashing daggers at him. "Lisa," she shouted up at him. "My name is Lisa and for someone who's just been on a wild merry-go-round ride, I am being damn reasonable. I don't know what you thought you were doing or why you thought you had to play some kind of cloak-and-dagger game with me, but guess what? Game over," she declared.

Finished, she turned on her heel and stormed over

to where she'd left her car. She made it to within five feet of the vehicle before Ian caught up to her. Grabbing hold of her arm, he quickly turned her around to face him. He just couldn't let her walk away from him like this. He had to make her understand.

"I was going to tell you today," he insisted. "Remember? I said I had something to tell you. That was it. That I was a writer. That I was B. D. Brendan." The look in her eyes told him it was too late. But he refused to accept that. "You have to give me a chance to explain."

Lisa struggled to pull back her wrist, then stopped.

"No," she told him between clenched teeth, "I don't. The time to have explained all that was *before* I found out what an idiot I was. Before I found out that for some reason, you didn't trust me."

A thousand things were going on in his brain. Pleas, appeals, explanations. He didn't follow what she was telling him. "Trust you?"

"To know your secret identity, *Superman.*" Lisa spat out the words, then yanked her wrist out of his grasp.

Before he knew it, she'd made it to her car and got in. She slammed the door shut and quickly locked all four automatically. He was pulling on the door handle, but it did no good. Keeping her eyes straight ahead, afraid that if she looked at him, she'd cry, Lisa put her car in gear and drove.

Ian was yelling her name and knocking on her window as he ran along the side of the car. She wouldn't allow herself to even glance in his direction. She needed to get away.

He stopped running just beyond the edge of the parking lot. She'd picked up speed and merged as far to the left as possible, cutting him off from any further pursuit unless he wanted to risk being hit by a car.

Stunned, angry, devastated, he walked back to his vehicle. Dan was standing beside it, the door on the driver's side wide open. So was the one on the passenger's side. Seeing him approach, Dan snapped to attention. He'd been a silent witness to it all.

"Want me to drive after her, Mr. Malone?" Even as he asked, he was getting in.

He did, Ian thought. With all his heart he did. He wanted to catch up to her, to corner her and make her listen to him.

But he knew better. This wasn't the time.

Ian sighed and shook his head. "No. In my experience, when someone's that angry, it's best just to let them cool off." The smile that slipped across his lips was self-deprecating. "Otherwise, vital parts of my anatomy might suddenly go missing."

He leaned into the driver's side of the car and popped the trunk. Since he was here, he might as well finish what he'd set out to do. Making his way to the rear of the vehicle, he took out two shopping bags and passed them to the driver, then took out two more. "C'mon, give me a hand with these, Dan. We have presents to put under the tree."

Susan held her tongue for as long as she could. But she'd never been known for her ability to just stand on the sidelines. And Lisa's suddenly erratic behavior had her concerned.

Lisa had come home earlier than expected from the shelter. Not only that, but as she sailed through the front door, she'd declared that they were leaving for the cabin now instead of tomorrow morning, as originally planned. Since everything was packed, it didn't seem like a problem.

To everyone but Susan.

She'd watched Lisa move upstairs and down like an amazon warrior in a video game. It didn't take a brain surgeon to figure out something was wrong.

"Aren't we going to wait for Ian?" Susan asked when Lisa stopped moving long enough for her to pose the question. "Or is he meeting us there?" But even as she asked the question, she had the sinking feeling she knew the answer.

Lisa placed the second set of suitcases by the front door, beside the first. "No and no."

"No?" Her daughter was going up the stairs again. This time, Susan decided to follow. "What happened?"

"Change of plans, Mother," Lisa threw over her shoulder.

Hand on the bottom of the banister, Susan stopped following. "Uh-uh."

Lisa turned her head to look at her. "What?"

Susan frowned. This was worse than she'd thought. "Every time you call me *Mother*, you're either angry at me or hurting."

She hated being transparent. She'd thought she was better at hiding her feelings by now. "I'm not angry at you," Lisa snapped.

Susan let the tone roll right off her back. "Then you're hurting."

Lisa bit her tongue to keep from saying something now that she'd regret later. Instead, in a patient voice, she said, "This isn't the time to exercise your policewoman muscles, Mothe—Mom."

Susan remained where she stood, looking up at her daughter's face. Wishing she had the power to wave a wand and make everything right.

"This has nothing to do with being a policewoman or former policewoman," she amended. "This has to do with being your mother. Now what happened and why isn't Ian coming with us?"

It was as if something suddenly drained out of her. Lisa sank down on the step above her mother and pulled her knees up to her chest. "Because he's a fraud."

Susan dropped down beside her daughter. "As in a con artist?"

Lisa moved her shoulders in a vague shrug. "In a manner of speaking."

Susan slipped a sympathetic arm around her daughter's shoulder. "You're going to have to give me more than that to work with."

No, she wasn't twelve anymore. Lisa straightened, pulling herself together. "Mother, with all due respect, this doesn't concern you."

Susan laughed softly, shaking her head. "Generally, when people say *with all due respect*, there usually isn't any." She gave a little shrug that was identical to the one her daughter had executed moments ago. "But we'll let that go for now. This concerns you and you concern me. If A equals B and B equals C, then—"

"A equals C," Lisa concluded wearily. And then she smiled affectionately at the woman beside her. "Just my luck to have the only math-oriented policewoman on the squad as my mother."

Susan's green eyes crinkled. "You always were lucky."

Lisa hugged her knees in harder. "Not hardly." She wanted to leave it at that, to swallow the pain and just keep moving. But she knew her mother was waiting for more and the penetrating stare was just too much for her. "He's a bestselling author."

Susan's eyes narrowed as she tried to follow what her daughter was saying. "Who?"

"Ian," Lisa cried impatiently, then waved her hand dismissively. "Or whatever his name is."

Susan chewed on this latest bit of rather surprising information. "A bestselling author instead of an idle rich man." She peered at Lisa's face. "And this bothers you because—?"

How could her mother miss this point? "Don't you see? He *lied* to me. He let me think he was some pampered socialite."

Susan was having a hard time seeing the downside of this. "Instead of a bestselling author."

She'd expected to have her mother on her side in this, but she could hear the barely-veiled amusement in Susan's voice. "He didn't trust me to know who he was. Didn't trust me to—oh damn, never mind." She rose to her feet on the step. "Please, can we just go?"

Susan rose as well. "Whatever you say. But I think you're making a mistake."

Lisa hurried up the stairs to move Casey along. He was still trying to decide which toys to take or, rather, which ones to leave behind. "You're allowed to think whatever you want, Mothe—Mom," she amended again, mentally upbraiding herself. "It's a free country."

Susan's mind was furiously working toward a resolution. She turned and walked back toward the front door. "It is indeed."

Lisa was in too much of a hurry to get out on the road to pick up on the shift in her mother's tone.

* * *

For the next day and a half, Lisa tried very hard, for Casey's sake, to be upbeat. But it was hard to be that way when her heart was missing in action because it had been shattered into a million little pieces. She'd honestly thought that Ian was the one. The man she might have a shot at happiness with. The man who had already created happiness within her.

Showed what she knew, she thought darkly. She was just going to have to hold a tighter rein on her emotions, that was all. Keep going, keep busy. God knew that wasn't hard.

She'd been a whirlwind of activity since they'd gotten here: buying and putting up the Christmas tree, decorating the cabin, cooking, baking, in essence remaining in perpetual motion as she desperately tried to outrun her thoughts.

But even so, thoughts of Ian were preying on her mind. Giving her no peace by rerunning moments in her head, making her think of him. Her thoughts were even playing tricks on her.

Like right now.

That man who was heading up the winding path from the road below, she could swear that he walked just like Ian. *Looked* just like Ian. Which was impossible. She hadn't told him where in Big Bear the cabin was located or even who it belonged to so there was no way that he could possibly track her down.

And yet—

"Omigod," she whispered, stunned.

The next moment, she was racing back into the house and down the stairs.

But she didn't beat Casey, who was already flying out the front door, forgetting to put his jacket on, tripping through the snow to get to the man who was approaching their cabin.

"You came, you came!" he cried, hurling himself into Ian's arms and nearly knocking him down. "Mama said you weren't gonna, but you came!"

"I came." Ian laughed. The next moment, he was picking the boy up and hugging him almost as hard as Casey was hugging him.

Lisa tried very hard to ignore the way the scene tugged on her heart. She struggled to remind herself that she couldn't trust a man who didn't tell her the truth. The fact that she wanted to fling herself into his arms just as Casey had was just something she was going to have to deal with.

"Casey, get into the house," she ordered sternly, taking possession of her son and leading him away from Ian. "You know you shouldn't be out here without your jacket on."

Casey twisted around in her arms. "But you're not wearing one, Mama."

"Don't argue with her, Case," Ian told him, coming closer. "Go inside and get your jacket. Your mom's got her anger to keep her warm."

Casey ran up the steps two at a time.

"You bet I do," Lisa retorted, her eyes blazing. "How did you know where to find us?" she demanded.

He'd missed her. He hadn't thought it was possible to miss anyone but his family so much, but he had. "I could say I moved heaven and earth to locate you, but that would be lying."

The muscle in her cheek twitched. "Something you're good at."

He decided to tell her the truth and let the chips fall where they would. "Your mother called me." Ian took another step closer to her, his eyes on hers. "And I never lied to you."

Her mouth nearly fell open. The feeling of betrayal throbbed in her chest. Couldn't she trust anyone? "My mother?" She turned just as she heard the front boards creak behind her.

Susan was standing just past the front doorway, her arms crossed before her as a barrier against the winds that were picking up.

"I thought that one of the Kittridge women should be sensible." And then she smiled as she looked at the young man standing in front of her daughter. "Besides, I never met a bestselling author."

"Fine, then you talk to him," Lisa retorted, storming away from both of them and the house. She ran toward the wooded area.

"Well, move, boy," Susan instructed, giving him

a shove in the right direction. "Before she freezes to death."

Ian nodded. "Thanks for all your help."

"Just go!"

Ian hurried after the reason he'd come all this way by a cab whose meter was still running.

He caught up to her before she'd gotten too far into the woods. Striping off his jacket, he draped it over her shoulders. She shrugged it off and he pushed it back on, closing the top button to keep her from shedding it again. "I never lied to you," he repeated.

She glared at him. "Omission is just as much of a lie as telling someone something that wasn't true. You let me go on thinking you were just a rich, self-centered bastard."

His mouth twisted in an amused smile. "You were having so much fun, I didn't want to take that away from you."

"You're not going to get anywhere by being charming." And if he thought he was, he was sadly mistaken because she wasn't some airhead, ready to be taken in by a magnetic personality. She'd had a short period of delusion, but she was over that.

He looked at her, deadly serious. "Then I'll tell you the truth."

"Ah, something new for you."

He ignored the sarcasm. Maybe he had it coming.

At any rate it made her feel better and there was something to be said for that.

"I didn't tell you who I was because I liked the fact that you felt I was just a regular screw-up who needed saving. Because I was," he added seriously. "Before you, I was going down the toilet and there was no off switch, no way to stop." He paused. When she said nothing, he pushed on because there was no other weapon available in his arsenal. Only the truth. "When people find out who I am—when they find out about my 'other' self—" he clarified because that was the way he regarded the persona who was the author "—they either make snide remarks, or they fawn. I didn't want that getting in the way with us."

"There is no *us*," she told him.

He pretended not to hear her. "You asked me who the hell I was the other day. Well, until these last couple of months, I didn't know. But I wasn't B. D. Brendan, that was just someone I made up. The name's just a composite of my parents and my sister. Bruce, Donna and Brenda. B. D. Brendan," he repeated. "I've never told anyone that before," he confided. "I *am* Ian Malone. A very wretched person who was alone until he met this feisty, stubborn teacher with a neat kid and an attitude problem." The smile faded from his lips. "You made me want to be a better person." He took her hands in his and to his relief, she didn't pull them away. "I *am* a better person because of you. I don't phone in my performances anymore, I show up. It's my life and I show up." She had to understand what a huge deal that was. "You brought me back to life. I'm even writing again because of you."

He looked into her eyes, offering her his soul, his secrets. "These last nine months, I lost the only thing I still had. I lost my ability to write. Morning after morning, I'd show up and sit down in front of my computer and I'd sit there, alone, without a thought in my head. The words didn't show up. You got the words to come back, Lisa. You got the words to come back. But none of it means anything if *you* don't come back."

He waited, out of breath, out of hope.

She took a long, deep breath and looked up into his eyes for a long moment without saying anything. And then she told him quietly, "Kitty." And then she smiled. "My name is Kitty."

Relief washed over him. "I thought you hated me calling you that."

She had, although looking back, she really couldn't say why. "In light of the circumstances, I've changed my mind."

The wind continued to pick up, but he was far too consumed with what was going on to notice. "Then it's all right? You're not angry at me anymore?"

She inclined her head and tried to keep a straight face. "That depends."

"On what?"

And then she allowed a smile to break through.

"On whether or not you dedicate the book you're working on to me."

"The book, my life, anything." He drew her into his arms. "I love you, Kitty."

She settled in against his arms, feeling warm. Feeling happy. "Because I made the words come back?"

The words were only a small part of it. She brought the sun in with her. "Because you made my soul come back. Marry me, Kitty?"

The simple question stunned her. "Wow, you pull out all the stops, don't you?"

"Too fast?" He was overwhelming her. He needed to go more slowly, but now that he had an inch, he wanted a mile. It was the nature of the beast. "You don't have to answer right away, you can—"

"Yes," she told him with enthusiasm.

He felt like a man in a dream, afraid of waking up. "Yes?"

"Yes." She grinned. "The answer's yes." She threaded her arms around his neck. "Because I love you, too. I have for a while now, I just didn't want to. But it seems I have no choice."

He breathed a huge sigh of relief. "Thank God." Releasing her, he took her hand and began to lead her down the hill. "C'mon."

She tried to pull him in the opposite direction, certain that he had just gotten turned around. "Ian, we're going down the path. The house is the other way."

But he shook his head. "I know, but I've got a cab down there with the meter running and a trunk full of presents."

She'd been frugal all of her life by necessity. All she could think of was what a huge waste of money that had to be. "How long has it been running?"

"Since I got here."

And then a surge of joy surprised Lisa as it burst over her. "Can it run a little longer?"

He looked at her over his shoulder, not sure where she was going with this. "Sure."

"Good. Because you forgot to kiss me when you proposed."

Ian stopped and turned around so suddenly that she nearly fell into his arms. "Kitty, I will never forget to kiss you again. Starting now."

And he didn't.

* * * * *

If you enjoy novels by Marie Ferrarella,
don't miss her next one!
Remodelling the Bachelor,
the start of THE SONS OF LILY MOREAU
mini-series, is out in June 2008!

Turn the page for a sneak preview of
Just Friends? *by Allison Leigh,*
coming to the shops in May 2008.

We think you'll love it!

Just Friends?

by

Allison Leigh

It didn't turn out at all the way Evan had intended.

When it started out, it was just supposed to be a quick trip home during a break between classes. He'd known she'd be home, too, because he'd made a point of finding out. Subtly, of course. It had never paid to show one's cards too easily where Leandra Clay was concerned. She was too quick. Too smart.

Too...everything.

Fool that he was, though, in his determination to appear *any*thing but obvious, he'd invited his dorm-mate.

Jake sure in hell hadn't worried about being subtle.

One look at Leandra and he'd been a goner.

Evan's fault. If he'd told Jake he'd already staked out that territory, his buddy wouldn't have trespassed.

Problem was, Leandra hadn't been Evan's territory. *Never* had been.

So what had Evan done?

Nothing.

And now what was Evan doing?

Nothing.

Nothing except stand there in his suit and a tie that felt like it was strangling him, and lift his champagne glass the way all the other wedding guests were lifting theirs.

"To the bride and groom," he managed to say. "We wish them a lifetime of happiness."

Jake wore a tux, too, and Leandra looked like some princess out of a storybook in filmy white stuff from head to toe. Their arms were slung around each other, giddy grins on their faces.

They'd hardly let go of each other in the year since Evan had introduced them.

The couple drank to the toast, and to the others that followed, kissed softly, sweetly, and Evan turned away, downing the rest of his champagne. But no amount of alcohol was going to deaden the pain inside him.

He hadn't spoken his piece when he should have.

"Hey, you." Leandra had untangled herself from Jake and touched Evan's arm. "Don't go running off now. You've got to promise me a dance after Jake and I do our thing."

He had to steel himself against flinching. "I was just going to find more of your dad's fine bubbly."

Her gaze, as rich as the fudge pudding Evan's mom had made since his childhood, was sparkling and that sparkle was all for her brand-spanking-new husband. "I'm not sure I ever said thank you. You know. For introducing Jake and me. If it hadn't been for you, we'd have never met."

"What are friends for?"

She missed the dark note in his voice. Nothing in her world right now was dark.

She was Leandra Clay and she'd just married the man of her dreams.

She suddenly reached out and hugged him. A quick dip into sweet perfume and soft, rustling white gown. "Thanks." Then she was moving away again, heading back to Jake, never knowing that she was taking Evan's heart along with her.

No, things definitely hadn't turned out at all the way he'd planned.

MILLS & BOON
Special Edition

On sale 18th April 2008

Just Friends?
by *Allison Leigh*

When producer Leandra Clay enlisted her old friend, rugged, sexy, *single* Evan Taggart, to be on her reality TV series, it was a good idea – they were both known to throw themselves into their work. But soon they were throwing themselves into each other's arms…until they found themselves fending off Evan's female fans!

One Man's Family
by *Brenda Harlen*

When Alicia Juarez turned to private eye Scott Logan to help get her brother out of trouble, the ex-cop had doubts. But it only took a little while before the pretty nurse with a fierce commitment to her brother and his two kids convinced Logan to take the case…and a chance on love.

Her Kind of Cowboy
by *Pat Warren*

Jesse Calder had promised to return to Abby Martin five years ago. Now, a horrible accident, lies and secrets stood between them, but Jesse could not ignore the spark that still lingered. Or forget that Abby's little girl had eyes a familiar shade of blue…

Having the Cowboy's Baby
by Stella Bagwell

The last thing Southern belle Anne-Marie Duveuil needed was to fall for another good-looking, sweet-talking man. But when Cordero Sanchez rode into town, the sparks flew, and soon a special surprise had them rethinking their vow not to exchange vows…

Falling for the Heiress
by Christine Flynn

Assigned to Tess Kendrick and her son, bodyguard Jeff Parker had no sympathy for Tess when he thought she was just a spoiled rich girl. But when Jeff learned of her true sacrifice to save the family name from her blackmailing ex, he knew he would do anything to protect this woman and child.

Sawyer's Special Delivery
by Nicole Foster

Paramedic Sawyer Morente's instinctive need to protect the child he's just brought into the world is at odds with Maya Rainbow's, the baby's mother's, determination to raise her son alone. Can Sawyer make Maya understand that he can heal her heart?

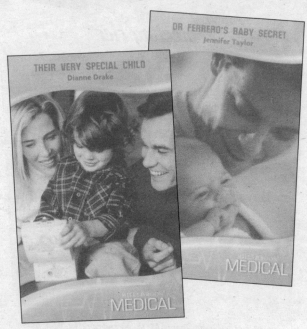

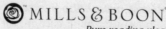

Celebrate 100 years
of pure reading pleasure
with Mills & Boon®

To mark our centenary, each month we're publishing a special 100th Birthday Edition. These celebratory editions are packed with extra features and include a FREE bonus story.

Plus, starting in February you'll have the chance to enter a fabulous monthly prize draw. See 100th Birthday Edition books for details.

Now that's worth celebrating!

15th February 2008

Raintree: Inferno by Linda Howard
Includes FREE bonus story Loving Evangeline
*A double dose of Linda Howard's heady mix
of passion and adventure*

4th April 2008

The Guardian's Forbidden Mistress by Miranda Lee
Includes FREE bonus story The Magnate's Mistress
*Two glamorous and sensual reads from favourite
author Miranda Lee!*

2nd May 2008

The Last Rake in London by Nicola Cornick
Includes FREE bonus story The Notorious Lord
*Lose yourself in two tales of high society and
rakish seduction!*

Look for Mills & Boon 100th Birthday Editions at
your favourite bookseller or visit
www.millsandboon.co.uk

4 FREE

BOOKS AND A SURPRISE GIFT!

We would like to take this opportunity to thank you for reading this Mills & Boon® book by offering you the chance to take FOUR more specially selected titles from the Special Edition series absolutely FREE! We're also making this offer to introduce you to the benefits of the Mills & Boon® Reader Service™—

- ★ **FREE home delivery**
- ★ **FREE gifts and competitions**
- ★ **FREE monthly Newsletter**
- ★ **Exclusive Reader Service offers**
- ★ **Books available before they're in the shops**

Accepting these FREE books and gift places you under no obligation to buy, you may cancel at any time, even after receiving your free shipment. Simply complete your details below and return the entire page to the address below. You don't even need a stamp!

YES! Please send me 4 free Special Edition books and a surprise gift. I understand that unless you hear from me. I will receive 6 superb new titles every month for just £3.15 each, postage and packing free. I am under no obligation to purchase any books and may cancel my subscription at any time. The free books and gift will be mine to keep in any case.

E8ZED

Ms/Mrs/Miss/Mr ....Initials ....
                                                                        BLOCK CAPITALS PLEASE
Surname ....

Address ....

....

....Postcode.............................

Send this whole page to:
UK: FREEPOST CN81, Croydon, CR9 3WZ